THE
SWITCH
UP

L.A. EXCHANGE

For Mike and Rich, with love

STRIPES PUBLISHING LIMITED
An imprint of the Little Tiger Group
1 Coda Studios, 189 Munster Road, London SW6 6AW

www.littletiger.co.uk

First published in Great Britain by Stripes Publishing Limited in 2020
Text copyright © Katy Cannon, 2020
Cover copyright © Stripes Publishing Limited, 2020
Cover images © Shutterstock.com

ISBN: 978-1-78895-192-0

The right of Katy Cannon to be identified as the author of this work has been
asserted by her in accordance with the Copyright, Designs and Patents Act, 1988.

A CIP catalogue record for this book is available from the British Library.

Printed and bound in the UK.

The Forest Stewardship Council® (FSC®) is a global, not-for-profit organization dedicated to
the promotion of responsible forest management worldwide. FSC® defines standards based on
agreed principles for responsible forest stewardship that are supported by environmental, social,
and economic stakeholders. To learn more, visit www.fsc.org

10 9 8 7 6 5 4 3 2 1

KATY CANNON

THE SWITCH UP

L.A. EXCHANGE

LiTTLE TiGER

LONDON

WILLA

Everything was perfect.

The lighting – natural Californian sunlight streaming between the buildings, illuminating my set. The setting – a quintessential all-American high school in Los Angeles, on the last day of term before spring break. The cast – giggling quietly just off camera, waiting for their big moment. The music – all queued up and ready to burst out of the speakers the instant I gave the signal. The camera angles – my friend Matty behind one camera, ready to get the static shots, and me darting in and out of the action with my trusty mini-camera, getting the really interesting views.

This was going to be *phenomenal*.

I'd been planning this day for months now, more or less since my second week at school here in LA. I wanted to create an *event*, the sort people would be talking about all through spring break, and beyond. I wanted to get noticed, in a way that my fledgling YouTube channel just hadn't achieved yet.

When Matty and I had been paired to work together on a small project at Film Club, we'd realized our styles melded well. Which was why I'd asked him to help me … and suddenly everything had come together.

There'd been a lot more to it, of course. People to persuade, rehearsals to schedule, blocking and planning and costumes and make-up … but finally we were there.

Today was the day I was going to make a real impression on my little corner of LA. Today, St Saviour's High School; tomorrow, the movie studios! Or, at least, *some* recognition.

"In five, four, three," I whispered into the mic linked to my assistant's earpiece. She watched me carefully from over where the cast were waiting as I held up two fingers, then one, then gave her the nod.

The music blasted out from the front steps of the school and over the grass verges, loud enough to be heard all the way to the far end of the car park. Students passing by looked up, some confused, some smiling. On the beat, my first few dancers emerged from their hiding places, their coordinated costumes and moves spectacular in the sunlight. With a quick glance to check that Matty was capturing the action in a wide shot, I darted into the dance to get the close-up shots.

We'd rehearsed this to the second and everyone knew exactly what they were supposed to do. As the beat changed, five students who'd seemingly just been hanging around the steps suddenly jumped up and started jiving, fast and furious, to the music.

It was just as I'd planned it. Right down to the cartwheels over the cars parked by the main hall, and the dancing on the edges of the concrete planters. I spun around in the middle of it all, catching the carefully coordinated chaos on film. Around us, people were laughing, clapping, cheering – even joining in. It was everything I'd dreamed it would be.

Right up until the moment I saw Principal Carter stalking across the grass towards me.

ALICE

Everything was horrible.

OK, fine, not everything, not all the time. But right now, as I hid in the girls' toilets at school, waiting for everyone else to leave, things felt pretty horrible.

I wasn't *supposed* to be in the girls' toilets. I was supposed to be at Climate Change Club, in the science classrooms. But it was the last day of the spring term, and no one else had even bothered to show up. Not that many people had shown up most of the other weeks this term either. Some days it was just me and Miss Morris, the teacher who ran the group.

This week, even Miss Morris had gone home early.

I always watched the climate protests on the telly, saw teenage activists across the world speaking on social media, yet I couldn't even get *my* school to change the name of the club to Climate Crisis Club. News reporters told me that my generation were fired up about climate change but apparently 'my generation' didn't go to Bollingsdale High School.

At my old school, we had recycling drives and

designed awareness posters and no one got in too much trouble for skipping school to attend the march in central London. I went with Dad and his girlfriend, Mabel, and the whole day was incredible – being surrounded by people who cared about the same things I did.

Basically the opposite of my new school.

When Dad and I moved from Cambridge to London in January, I tried to think of it as an adventure. I was happy that he'd got a new job at the university where Mabel worked. But living in Mabel's tiny flat until we found a new home, taking the Tube to school every day instead of riding my bike, and sleeping with the noise of London outside my window took a lot of adjusting to. And then there was school.

Bollingsdale was a good school – great reputation, outstanding inspection reports, higher than average exam results. Dad never stopped telling me how lucky we were that I was able to get in there. And I was sure it was a good school for lots of people.

Just not for me.

I didn't fit in there. I didn't want to be there – and from what I could tell, the other students didn't want me there either. Everyone already had their group of friends – I mean, they'd had fourteen or fifteen years to sort that out.

I tried to go to an after-school club most days, because that meant leaving later than everyone else. To be precise, it meant leaving later than Cassidy, Mollie and Jana, the three girls in my year who seemed to get a peculiar joy out of making me miserable.

"Alice?"

My name echoed around the empty room and I smiled. OK, fine, maybe there was *one* person in the whole school who didn't mind me being there.

"Hal, you are definitely not allowed in the girls' toilets," I told him as I unlocked the cubicle door.

He was standing in the doorway, waiting for me. "I'm not in. I'm hovering on the boundary. Plus you're hiding and I want to get home, so come on!"

Hal spent last summer helping my best friend Willa pretend to be me (long story) and they became pretty good friends. I think she must have told him to keep an eye out for me because ever since I started at Bollingsdale, he'd checked in on me most days. He had his own friends but he still made time for me, walking me to and from the Tube station nearest our school. I appreciated that a lot. Willa said he had a crush on me, but I didn't believe her.

Grabbing my bag, I followed him out and we headed for the Tube together.

"When do you leave for LA?" he asked as we walked along the busy London pavements.

"Tomorrow morning." I had my bags packed, my passport and paperwork triple-checked, and a book already picked out for the plane.

"Are you excited?"

"Very." This time tomorrow I'd be almost there – in fact, by LA time, I *would* be there! I'd be in Hollywood, with Willa, a world away from Bollingsdale. Me and my best friend, relaxing in the sunshine and having fun for two whole weeks. I couldn't wait.

"Just don't let her talk you into anything crazy this time, yeah?" Hal joked.

I laughed. "I think we used up all our craziness last summer! We'll probably just go to the beach and stuff."

Which was true. But I couldn't stop a small part of me hoping there might be a touch of Willa's unique mayhem about my trip. Because I couldn't deny that last summer had been *fun*. And I hadn't had a lot of fun lately. I thought about how, if I had been pretending to be Willa, Bollingsdale wouldn't be nearly so bad. Willa wouldn't care what other people thought about her. And when *I'd* been Willa last summer, I'd had some of that magic confidence too.

Maybe hanging out with her for a fortnight would help me find it again.

WILLA

So it turns out that school is school, wherever you are.

When my mum's contract got extended, and she told me we'd be staying in California for at least a year, I thought that going to school in LA would be the best. I mean, I'd be living and studying in Hollywood. I'd be starting September as a 'freshman' in high school. I'd seen the teen TV dramas, not to mention the reality shows. Finally I'd be living and learning somewhere that *got* me, Willa Andrews, star in the making. This was the place where all my dreams of becoming a famous director (who perhaps starred in her own films) would come true.

Except apparently, when you organize a student flash mob to perform near the car park and one or two cars get a little dinged, and the presentations the tenth-grade students were being tested on get a tiny bit disturbed, nobody praises your directorial ability...

No, instead I just got hauled to the principal's office. Which felt exactly the same as being dragged into the headteacher's office back at home.

My mum sat statue-like beside me as we waited for Principal Carter to pass judgement. She'd already had a long talk with him while I kicked my heels outside, waiting my turn. I could predict exactly what he was going to say – the same as all my other annoyed headteachers.

We'd already done the 'very disappointed, not the behaviour we expect from a St Saviour's student' spiel. He'd thrown in an 'appreciate you're still adjusting to a new country as well as a new school, and it's good that you're making friends and joining in', which I thought was nice. Unfortunately it was followed by a 'but behaviour of this nature cannot go unpunished, especially when the grades of other students are involved.'

So now we were just waiting to find out exactly what that punishment was.

Great.

I could almost hear Alice's voice in my head, telling me that I should have planned it better. If I'd only held the flash mob *after* school, or somewhere else. But that would have missed the point. It had to be at school, and during school hours, or no one would have seen it – and what good would that be?

I might not be a planner like Alice, but that didn't

mean I didn't have an end goal in mind. I'd joined the Film Club as soon as I started at St Saviour's, but I was a freshman, and just showing up every week and sharing my YouTube posts wasn't enough to get the older students to take notice. I wanted more. And I saw my chance: the Senior Film Class short film project. Last year, the film the class made had actually won awards and got some buzz. Everyone who worked on it got into film school and I wasn't willing to wait another two years to get that kind of experience. I wanted to do it *now*. This year, the hot ticket project was being directed by Fran Levine, the coolest senior in the school, who was already tipped as the Next Big Thing in local indie film circles. This was *absolutely* meant to be.

And working with Matty had given me the opportunity. I wanted him to put in a word for me. "Show me what you can do first," he'd said.

So I'd shown him.

See? I had a plan. I just had to get through whatever punishment Principal Carter dreamed up for me first.

Across the desk, he steepled his fingers and rested them against his lips. He was a big guy in a perfectly cut grey suit and, normally, I liked him. He sometimes played basketball and soccer with the students after school and showed up for every performance of the Glee Club, even joining in with a deep harmony now and then. I had a sneaking suspicion that, had it not been for the interruption of the oral presentations, he'd have *loved* my flash mob.

"Willa, over this spring break, what I would like is for you to work on thinking about others before you act." His dark brown eyes were serious. "So, I've had a discussion with your mother and we've come up with the following plan. This spring break, you're going to spend at least four hours every weekday volunteering at the Shore Thing Project. It's a charity venture the school is involved with."

"Sure thing?"

Mum shook her head. "The *Shore* Thing," she repeated, as if I could tell the difference in spelling from her pronunciation (which I couldn't). "It's run by my friend Darla down at Santa Monica Bay. They're working on cleaning up the shoreline around LA, and educating school children, locals and tourists on the importance of looking after our seas."

"The future of our planet is in all our hands," Principal Carter continued, "and people like the volunteers at the Shore Thing Project are really trying to take charge. A lot of our students are already involved as part of their environmental science studies, and Darla has agreed to let you volunteer there during the two-week break. I think it will be a real learning experience for you."

"Sounds ... great." Actually, it sounded incredibly boring. Or like something Alice would love. Or both.

Wait. Alice.

"Do I have to do it over spring break?" I asked, sitting up straight in my chair for the first time since the meeting started. "I mean, I get that it's really important, that I need to make amends, and think of others and all that ... but could I start thinking about others *after* spring break?"

Principal Carter barely hid his smile at that. "Willa, this is what your mother and I have agreed, to avoid a suspension on your permanent record."

"Right. It's just ... I have a friend visiting from England for spring break. I haven't seen her since last summer!"

"Alice's dad is a marine biologist," Mum reminded me. "I'm sure she'll love spending some time at the Shore Thing too."

"Fine." I slumped back in my chair. "I'll spend my spring break counting seahorses or whatever."

"Learning to think about others," Principal Carter

corrected me. "And how we're all equally important parts of the larger world around us. Even seahorses."

Mum got to her feet, shaking Principal Carter's hand. I followed her out of the office to the car. The rest of the school had already broken up and the car park was almost deserted.

Yeah, so I now had to spend forty hours volunteering at some seaside thing but I reckoned it was worth it for the footage I'd got. Tomorrow Alice would arrive, and I knew we'd still manage to have fun. Everything would be fine.

Mum gave me the silent treatment as I climbed into the car. From past experience, I figured that would probably wear off in time for her to read me the riot act over dinner. For now, I just enjoyed the peace.

My phone buzzed in my pocket and I pulled it out. It was a message from Matty.

Got you in on the project! Fran says we start filming Monday – it will be every day over spring break, except weekends. I'll swing by tomorrow and fill you in on the details. You owe me!

My eyes widened. Matty had come through for me! Everything I'd worked on so hard for weeks and weeks had been worth it – I'd be the only freshman involved with the best Senior Film Class project! That made even my punishment worthwhile.

Wait.

I re-read Matty's message. Filming was over spring break. Exactly when I was supposed to be volunteering at the Shore Thing project *and* showing Alice the LA sights.

Even *I* couldn't be in three places at once.

Could I?

ALICE

Heathrow airport was exactly as I remembered it from last summer. I just wished I still felt like the girl I'd been then, full of hope and confidence after spending a summer in Italy pretending to be Willa.

Right now, I felt every bit Alice again. Anxious, small and unsure.

Waiting in line to check in, while Dad located the Unaccompanied Minors person from the airline, I pulled my passport, ticket, journal and phone out of my bag one last time.

"I wouldn't imagine they'd have disappeared in the three minutes since you last checked them," Mabel commented, with a gentle smile.

I shoved my things back down again, feeling a blush hit my cheeks.

I liked my dad's girlfriend. I hadn't expected to, but I did. Maybe it was because I'd spent all of last summer avoiding her, only to find that she was just as nervous about meeting me as I was her. It helped that Willa had liked her too.

16

"I bet you're excited to see Willa again," Mabel said, obviously trying to find something to take my mind off my nerves.

"Yeah." I was. In fact, the invitation from Willa's mum to spend spring break with them was pretty much the only thing that had got me through the last term at school.

Maybe spending time with Willa would help me find *that* Alice again. The one who took risks. The Alice who had made good friends and learned a lot. I'd like to bring *that* Alice back to London when school started again.

"You must tell her all about your new school, and the house-hunting," Mabel went on. From the edge in her voice I could tell she was just talking for the sake of it, filling the silences. "And make sure she knows it's her turn to visit us next! I hope she can come in the summer, for the wedding."

Of course. The wedding. Dad and Mabel were getting married.

Woohoo.

No, I was being unfair. Dad and Mabel were happy together, and that made me happy too. Honestly.

Dad hurried back with a smiling woman in uniform. "Alice, this is Marta. She's going to look after you until you reach LA."

"Hi, Marta." I gave her a tentative smile.

"Don't you worry about anything, Alice," she said, beaming back at me. "I'll take very good care of you until you reach your friends in California."

I turned to Dad and Mabel to say my goodbyes. Suddenly there was a huge lump in my throat I hadn't expected. I *wanted* to go to LA and see Willa but I hated saying goodbye.

Dad hugged me tight then stepped back, holding on to my arms as he dipped his head so our noses were level. "Now, we'll call every night, yes?"

I nodded fiercely.

"And you absolutely won't swap places with a random stranger on your flight, right?" Marta looked a little alarmed at Dad's joke, but it made me smile.

"Not this time," I promised.

He let go and Mabel moved in to hug me goodbye. "Don't let Hollywood change you," she teased.

Dad joined the hug, and I felt enveloped in their love. "Too right," he said. "We love you just the way you are, Starfish."

I gave them a shaky smile and a wave as Marta led me away to the Unaccompanied Minors lounge.

Don't let Hollywood change you.

That was exactly what I *wanted* to happen. I wanted to come home from LA a different Alice. One who could fit in at school and stop hiding out in the toilets or the library. One who wouldn't lie in bed worrying. One who would fight for what mattered to her, even if it didn't matter to anyone else.

And now the goodbyes were out of the way, my excitement was starting to build again. A buzz, deep in my stomach, that was growing with my smile as I thought about two weeks in LA with Willa.

I checked my passport and ticket one last time. Still there.

I was ready.

WILLA

Why are all schools awful?

HAL

Hmm, YOU hate all schools, all schools find YOU difficult... If only there was a common denominator...

WILLA

Not helping.

HAL

No, just being hilarious.

WILLA

Amusing to an audience of one.

HAL

So what happened?

WILLA

Nobody appreciated my BRILLIANT flash-mob performance and now I have to volunteer every single day over spring break.

HAL

Ah. Is it up on YouTube?

WILLA

Check later tonight. You're going to love it.

HAL

I'm sure I will. Is Alice there yet?

WILLA

Arriving this afternoon. She doesn't know yet about the whole volunteering thing. But it's for some coastline conservation charity, so she'll probably love it.

HAL

That's good. She's finding it kind of hard here in London. I think she's looking forward to getting away.

WILLA

Hard how?

HAL

You know. Fitting in and stuff. She's kind of … quiet too.

WILLA

She's always quiet.

HAL

Not this sort of quiet. Just … look after her, yeah?

WILLA

Of course! Whatever's wrong, I can fix it. She's probably just stressing about her dad and Mabel's wedding or something.

HAL

Yeah, probably. So what else have you got planned for her visit, apart from volunteering?

WILLA

Funny you should ask. How do you think Alice would feel about another of my brilliant plans…?

WILLA

Because Alice was travelling as an unaccompanied minor, Mum had needed a letter from Alice's dad to say she was authorized to pick her up. I'd hoped it would mean we could meet her straight off the plane, but because she was travelling internationally we had to wait until after customs and immigration.

I practically fizzed with excitement as we zoomed through the airport. When we got to the spot where we expected her to appear, I jammed the chauffeur's hat I'd picked up at a costume store on my head and held up the sign I'd made with Alice's name on it. I hadn't seen her for almost nine months, and I was desperate for her to just get here already.

Would she have changed much? I mean, we'd texted and emailed and kept up on social media plenty but she hardly ever posted photos of herself. Would we even look alike any more? That was the one thing that had brought us together. It was hard to imagine her looking different to me now. I strained to spot her in the crowds coming through to the arrivals hall, mentally discounting people as they passed. *Too old, too young, too blond, too short…*

And then I saw her. Same long brown hair as me, same slim figure I remembered, her shoulders slightly hunched and her eyes tired.

But it was Alice.

I pushed through the tide of people to reach her and her face lit up, the tiredness I'd seen in her fading away. We hugged tightly, while Mum dealt with the Unaccompanied Minors person who'd brought Alice through.

"I can't believe you're really here!" I placed my cap on her head and she laughed.

"Neither can I! After last summer, I never thought my dad would let me on a plane again."

"It took some persuasion," Mum said drily. "But I promised to keep a close eye on the pair of you."

"I promised my dad and Mabel I'd be on my absolute best ever behaviour while I was here," Alice said fervently.

"Glad to hear it," Mum replied. "Now, come on. Let's find your bag and get you home."

Home, as I explained to Alice in the car, wasn't exactly ours.

"When we realized we were going to be staying

in LA longer than planned, Mum started house-hunting. Then Mum's friend Harrison said we could use his place, because he'd be over in London for the next twelve months anyway, starring in some musical in the West End."

"That was kind of him," Alice said.

"*Very* kind," Mum murmured from the driver's seat.

You see, Harrison's house wasn't just a house. It was a mansion. *Loads* bigger than our place back home in Cheshire, and located in one of the priciest areas in LA. The Brentwood house had six bedrooms, a pool, a huge garden and a den that was basically just mine. Dad had his own room when he came out to visit and my bedroom had two double beds in it.

My favourite bit about the house though was the patio by the pool, where there were loungers and sofas with big, soft cushions, a chest full of blankets for warming up after a dip, and even a fireplace for cooler evenings.

I'd considered telling Alice all about this before she arrived, but decided it would be more fun to see her face when she realized where she'd be staying.

"So, what do you have planned for while I'm here?" Alice asked. "I was reading up about all the sights on the plane. There's so much I want to do!"

Mum gave me a meaningful look in the rear-view mirror. I knew what it meant. It meant 'you have to tell Alice about the Shore Thing volunteering'.

And I absolutely would. Later.

"OK, so, we have to go shopping, obviously. And you have to see Hollywood Boulevard and its stars. And the beach! We're totally doing Santa Monica beach, repeatedly." Especially since we'd be right there volunteering anyway.

"Sounds fantastic," Alice said, smiling. Meanwhile, Mum's eyes narrowed further in the mirror. Really, she should have been watching the road, not me.

Mum turned off San Vicente Boulevard and on to our street. Alice's eyes widened as the houses we drove past grew bigger and bigger, until Mum pulled in at the gates to Harrison's mansion. Leaning out of the window, she punched the code into the security pad, and the gates swung open automatically.

"You're staying *here?*" Alice gasped. I was right: totally blown away.

"Yep." I grinned. "Welcome to your best holiday ever!"

ALICE

Willa's new house was, basically, a palace.

Climbing slowly out of the car, I attempted to take in the sheer size of the building. It was two storeys, but with red-tile roofs at different heights above the white walls, wrought iron balconies and arched terraces. It looked like it belonged on a Mediterranean hillside, down to the potted olive trees outside the front door.

Once we'd unloaded my suitcase, Willa's mum took the car round to the garage at the side, and Willa and I lugged my stuff up the two shallow steps to the terrace and the front door. I could smell something sweet and citrusy on the breeze and, when I looked around, saw actual orange trees growing in the garden.

"This place is incredible," I whispered to Willa.

"It's pretty awesome," she agreed, grinning. "And you haven't even seen the pool yet!"

Dumping my case at the bottom of a sweeping staircase, Willa led me straight through the immaculate lounge (also painted white, with white-tile floors and huge, squidgy-looking white sofas with azure blue cushions) and out to the back terrace.

The pool, shimmering blue in the afternoon sun, was fabulous. Kicking off my trainers and socks, I dipped my toe into the water; just warm enough for swimming. Perfect.

Already that small buzz of excitement I'd felt leaving London had grown until it seemed to fill me. I was here, in LA, in a *mansion,* ready for the best holiday of my life. It was almost unbelievable – except for the part where it was really happening.

Willa had disappeared by the time I turned round, but after a little searching I found her fetching drinks from a small bar set up on the pool terrace. She handed me a can of lemonade and we settled on to the oversized beanbag chairs, with a great view over the pool and to the mountains beyond.

"I feel like I'm in a different world," I admitted.

"You kind of are." Willa flashed me a grin. "I mean, I *love* London, but LA is something else, right? So, what's the news from home? Any gossip?"

I shook my head. "Not really. New school is, well, school. Having Hal there helps though."

Willa raised her eyebrows. "Oh?"

"Not like that. He's a friend, that's all. Um, Dad and Mabel are embarrassingly happy together, and constantly dragging me house-hunting. Oh, they're hoping you can come over for the wedding this summer, by the way."

Willa sat up straighter. "Definitely! I always love an excuse to go dress shopping. Plus, you know, I feel kind of responsible for their happily ever after."

"How do you work that one out?"

"Well, if I hadn't been such an awesome house guest pretending to be you last summer, Mabel might have been put off step-mumming for life, and then they'd never have even got engaged!"

I didn't point out that that had been the *actual* plan. Willa had a way of making the facts fit her own version of reality.

"What about here?" I asked. "How's your new school?"

I knew Willa had been hoping it would be some sort of a school for film stars, but as far as I could tell from her messages and emails it was just an ordinary school. Or at least, as ordinary as schools got in LA.

Willa drained the rest of her can, then jumped to her feet to dump it in the bin. "Like you say, school is school. Come on. Let's dig out your best bikini and go for a swim."

Before I even had a chance to tell her that I didn't

own a bikini, just an ordinary sporty swimsuit, Willa's mum appeared, followed by a boy and a girl who both looked a couple of years older than us.

"Willa, your friends are here." Mrs Andrews didn't look too happy about it. "But please don't forget that you and Alice have lots to sort out before tomorrow. And I'm sure she's tired after such a long flight."

I *had* been tired, but the exhaustion I'd felt when I'd got off the plane seemed to have evaporated in the Californian sunshine. Now I was here, I was just excited – excited to see Willa, to explore this place, to catch up. Not so excited to spend time with people I didn't know though.

"Matty!" Willa motioned the newcomers through to our little nest and sat down again. "And...?" She left it hanging, and I realized she didn't know who the girl was either.

"Oh, this is my girlfriend, Jenn." Matty dropped on to a spare beanbag as Jenn smiled weakly at us. "She'll be working with us too."

Working with us? On what? And am I *part of the 'us'?* Uncertainty started to replace my excitement again.

"This is my friend Alice, from London," Willa said, waving a hand vaguely in my direction.

Matty's eyebrows went up. "The one you switched places with?" He studied me for a moment, which I didn't like. "Wow. You guys really *do* look alike."

Jenn frowned. "You guys switched places?"

"Long story," Willa said dismissively. She leaned forwards with her elbows on her knees, folded almost double in the beanbag chair. "We have more important things to talk about. I'm really in?"

Matty nodded. "I spoke to Fran, talked you up. Told her I think you have real promise – so you better live up to expectations."

"I always do," Willa said, with a confidence that made me green with envy. "But … it has to be these two weeks?"

"Yeah, spring break is perfect. Mr Harris is going to let us use the school equipment and Principal Carter even said we can do some shooting at school on days when staff will be in. Add in the beach and a few shots in the park downtown for atmosphere, and that's the locations all sorted!"

Matty's excitement was palpable, and apparently catching, since Willa looked even more animated than she had when I arrived. Jenn, meanwhile, sat morosely to one side.

My own excitement at being in LA was seeping

away as I realized that Willa had committed to some student film project for the whole two weeks of my visit. One that was apparently far more exciting than our adventures last summer.

Where's the bright side, Alice?

My mum's familiar question floated through my head. Even though she'd died five years ago now, it was when difficult situations arose that I felt her closest to me, her voice a whisper at the back of my brain. She'd always encouraged me to look at any challenge from both sides, to consider the worst – and the best – that could happen. She said that you never knew which you were going to get until it happened, and most of the time both were equally likely.

So, where was my bright side? Maybe I'd get to work with Willa on the film project. It wasn't exactly my kind of thing, but then I'd never tried it before. Maybe I'd love it. I knew Willa did. People thought that Willa could be flaky, but when she really cared about something she stuck with it – and she cared about making films more than just about anything.

Mrs Andrews' head appeared through the open door again. "Willa? Pizza will be here in ten minutes."

Matty jumped to his feet. "We can't stop anyway. Jenn's working props for the film and there's loads we still need to collect."

"And practically no budget," Jenn added.

"We're all having to double up on jobs," Matty said. "Too many people away for spring break. So I'm locations and cameras and Jenn is props and—"

"General dogsbody," Jenn finished for him. "Same as you, I imagine." She smiled at Willa as she said the last bit, but it was more of a self-satisfied smile than a friendly one.

I really couldn't see Willa and Jenn getting along very well.

"I prefer 'production assistant'," Willa shot back. Yep, that was Willa. Rewriting reality to suit herself again.

We walked them to the front door, and I waited until they were gone to ask about the film. "So, when you said in your last email you had plans for my visit, this was what you were talking about?"

Willa shook her head. "This just came up yesterday. And don't worry, it's not like it will be an all-day every-day thing. We'll have plenty of time to hang out. Plus—"

But before I could find out what else she wanted to

say, the doorbell rang again and Willa yanked it open to reveal the pizza delivery guy.

"We'll talk later," she promised. "Don't worry about anything."

Except that was a lot easier said than done.

WILLA

"Have you told Alice about the Shore Thing Project yet?" Mum whispered sharply as I helped her open the pizza boxes.

I shook my head. "I want to let her settle in first." I hadn't wanted her to find out about the film yet, either, but Matty had a lousy sense of timing. And a really dull girlfriend; I wasn't looking forward to working with Jenn much. General dogsbody, indeed. Clearly she had no idea how brilliantly useful I was going to be on this project. I reckoned that Fran, the director, would find me indispensible by the end of the first day.

Mum glanced over at where Alice sat cross-legged on her chair at the kitchen table, reading a book she must have pulled from her bag. "She looks pretty settled to me."

"I suppose."

Giving me a gentle shove towards Alice, Mum said, "Leave the pizza to me. You go break the news so we can all enjoy a nice dinner without it hanging over us."

Reluctantly I shuffled over to the table at the other

end of the ridiculously large kitchen and sat next to Alice, who put a bookmark between the pages, closed the book and smiled up at me.

"So I need to talk to you about something that's happening this holiday," I said.

"It's OK," Alice said. "I mean, I was a bit surprised at first, but I've been thinking about it and actually—"

She thought I was still talking about the film! Which Mum definitely did *not* know about, and I needed to keep it that way. I widened my eyes dramatically and shook my head, silently mouthing 'no!' at Alice.

Her forehead furrowed in confusion, but she followed my lead all the same and changed tack.

"I'm fine with whatever you have planned?" It came out sounding like a question, but it was better than nothing, I supposed. I checked over my shoulder and Mum didn't seem to have noticed anything out of the ordinary.

"So, um, what exactly *will* we be doing this holiday?" Alice asked.

"Well, I know how much you love the ocean and the environment and all that stuff."

"You mean, the future of our planet and our continued existence?" Alice raised her eyebrows. "All *that* stuff?"

"Yeah! So, I've been spending a lot of time down at Santa Monica beach since we moved here, and it turns out there's a cleaner oceans charity thing there called the Shore Thing Project. You know, shore spelled s-h-o-r-e."

Alice grinned at the name. "Sounds great. So, we're going to visit them?"

"Better! We're going to volunteer there! For at least four hours every weekday of the holidays," I added, quoting Principal Carter.

Alice's eyes narrowed. I guess the 'four hours every weekday' bit was a little too specific. "When you say 'volunteer'…"

I sighed. "OK, fine, I *have* to go work there for a stupid school thing."

"A consequence of your actions!" Mum added from the other end of the kitchen. I wished she'd just bring the pizza over already. It would be going cold.

"And I thought you might like to come with me," I finished.

"Sounds fun," Alice said, with a shrug. Then she leaned closer and whispered, "But what about the film thing?"

Glancing back over my shoulder, I saw Mum approaching with pizza on actual plates – clearly a concession to the fact we had a guest; we normally just ate it out of the boxes. There was a salad on the counter too, which was probably why she'd taken so long.

"I'll explain later," I whispered back.

Alice stood up and went to fetch the salad for Mum. "So, come on. Tell me what you did to get lumbered with volunteering all holiday," she called from the counter.

I tipped my chair back on two legs so I could still see her without turning round. "Now *that* is a story. Alice, it was glorious."

Mum groaned as she sat down. "That's one word for it. Sit up properly, Willa."

"Wait until I show you the video," I told them, lowering the front legs of my chair back to the ground with a crack. "You're both going to love it."

Dinner was fun. I liked sitting at the kitchen table with Alice and Mum – it made a change from our usual evenings, when Mum and I ate in silence while she read her script for the following day or checked her social-media accounts, and I messaged my friends. Tonight was like messaging with Alice, only better, because she was actually here – and it was even nice to have Mum chipping in from time to time. Her call schedule for the TV series she was working on varied from day to day, so some mornings she was gone before I woke up and other days she wasn't back before I went to bed. Some days we communicated exclusively through notes stuck to the ginormous fridge-freezer.

Of course, that meant that when we *did* have time together, she tried to double down on the 'being the perfect mum' thing. Which was even worse.

"I hope you don't mind about the Shore Thing Project, Alice," she said, when I'd finished showing the film of my epic school flash mob to them both. "When Principal Carter suggested it as a suitable challenge for Willa, I thought at least it was something you might find interesting as well."

Alice nodded with a lot more enthusiasm than I felt about the whole thing. "It sounds really great. I can't wait to find out more."

"Well, tomorrow is Sunday, but my friend Darla who runs the place said I could take you both down there to get the lay of the land before you start on Monday, if you like?"

"That would be great!" Alice replied, before I had a

chance to think of a reason why we couldn't.

Hmm. That was going to give us less time to iron out the details of my cunning plan – a plan I'd started working on while we were waiting at the airport for Alice. Still, I was sure Alice and I could figure it all out if we worked together.

First, I just had to get Alice to agree. And if I could do that, the rest would be simple.

ALICE

Californian takeaway pizza probably tasted pretty much the same as London takeaway pizza, but sitting with Willa and her mum to eat it made it seem even more delicious. It would have been more fun if Willa hadn't been giving me conspiratorial looks through the whole thing though. I was surprised her mum didn't notice. I mean, Willa thinks she's subtle but actually she's really easy to read. So I already knew, before she whispered "I've got a plan" to me as I dragged my suitcase up the wide, twisting staircase to her room, that she was up to something.

"I promised my dad and Mabel I absolutely wouldn't get into any trouble this holiday," I said, the moment Willa closed the bedroom door behind us. "Like, Dad actually made me stand there and repeat after him, 'I promise I won't get into any trouble with Willa this holiday' before he'd book my plane tickets."

"I'm not going to get you into any trouble!" Willa gave off the impression of being offended I'd even imagine such a thing. Which only made me more nervous.

"Are you going to get *you* into trouble?" I asked.

"Technically, no. Not if you help me." Willa bounced on to the bed beside me, grinning. "Look, here's the thing. Before the whole flash mob punishment thing happened yesterday, my only plans for this holiday were hanging out with you. But then Principal Carter hauled me and Mum into his office, and the next thing I know I have volunteering duties every day. And *then,* just as we're heading home, I get a text from Matty about the film."

The film. That was the part I *really* didn't understand. "Tell me about the film thing."

"OK, so, the Senior Film Class at my school does a big end of year project and it's always *stellar*. Like, they enter it in festivals and competitions, and sometimes they even win."

"But you're not a senior. Right?" I only had a vague understanding of how the American school system worked, mostly gained from bingeing high-school drama series on Netflix, but I was pretty sure that seniors were, well, more senior than us.

"No. But Matty is." Willa bounced off her knees and sat cross-legged across from me instead. The determined gleam in her eye sent me right back to sitting next to her on a plane last summer. Whatever Willa wanted this time, she *really* wanted it. "He's also in the school Film Club with me – he helped with the flash mob, actually, not that I told Principal Carter that. I needed to prove to Matty that I really know what I'm doing when it comes to film."

"So the flash mob was kind of your audition?" I was starting to see where this was going.

"Exactly! Ages ago, I asked him if he could get me in on the Senior Film Class project – I want to do a kind of behind-the-scenes documentary thing, you see."

"I thought Jenn said you were going to be a general dogsbody."

Willa waved that thought away with a hand. "What does Jenn know? She's not even in the Senior Film Class, *or* in Film Club. I don't understand why she wants to be involved – although I heard someone at Film Club saying that Jenn only got interested in film when she started dating Matty, and she only cares about the project because she's suspicious about him being close with Fran, the director. Who is beyond awesome, by the way."

"The director?" I asked, just to make sure I was following everything correctly.

"Yeah! She's super talented and comes up with all these really cool projects. If I can prove myself to her, I might get to work on more of them, even after she graduates."

"Makes sense." If you were Willa, anyway.

"So I figure, I'll make myself indispensible to Fran *and* get to film my behind-the-scenes documentary. Which will be the perfect audition video for getting into the Senior Film Class next year!"

"You seem to have thought it all out," I admitted.

Willa deflated suddenly, lowering her chin as her shoulders drooped. "Apart from the bit where they decided to film over spring break. So now I need to be in three places at once for the next two weeks – on the film set, at the Shore Thing Project and hanging out with you." She peeked up at me from under her lashes and I realized that this was all part of her plan. She was pretending to be totally disheartened so I'd agree to whatever crazy scheme she'd come up with.

Well, I wasn't going to make it that easy for her.

"At least doing the Shore Thing Project together means we'll be able to hang out at the same time. So that's two of your three things. It's a shame you won't be able to do the film, but it's better than nothing, right?"

Willa's gaze shot up to meet mine and she dropped the whole 'poor little me' act, which was a relief. It *really* didn't suit her.

"What if there was a way I *could* do everything?"

"Did you find a Time Turner down at Santa Monica Bay?" I asked.

"Better." Willa grinned. "I found you."

I shook my head. Given our adventures last summer, I knew exactly where this was going.

"It'll be fun, I promise. And really, we won't be doing anything wrong, so you can't possibly get into trouble!"

Somehow, I doubted that. But all the same, that strange spark of excitement was growing again in my stomach.

Willa grabbed her tablet from the desk, along with a map of LA. "OK, so Matty has sent me the locations for all the film shoots, right? The Shore Thing is there." She spread the map out across the floor and pointed to a building on the Santa Monica beach. "And we're filming…" She checked her tablet. "There, there and there. The park, school and on the beach itself."

"You want to try to do both?" I guessed.

Willa gave me a wicked grin. "Principal Carter just said that I had to volunteer four hours a day at the project. He never said *which* four hours. So I figure, we get there early, do a couple of hours, race off to the set and do a day of filming, then head back to do the last couple of hours at the Shore Thing before bed!"

Already I had a feeling that this wasn't going to work.

"How long does it take to get from Santa Monica to the school?" I asked.

"Depends on traffic. About half an hour? As long as you're not doing it at rush hour."

Taking the tablet from her, I opened up the Shore Thing Project website. "OK, so their offices open at nine and close at five most nights unless there's an evening event. So if we worked there until eleven, we'd get to the filming by eleven thirty—"

"Apart from the days it's at the park," Willa said. "That's about another fifteen minutes."

"Say twelve to allow for traffic," I continued. "Stay there until two, then head back to Santa Monica by three, do another two hours, then go home."

"That's only two hours a day on set!" Willa objected. "It's not going to work." Which was kind of my point. She sounded so despondent, I felt bad for being the one to tell her. I could see how much this film project meant to her, and I wanted her to do it. But we couldn't be in two places at once.

Which seemed ridiculous. I mean, we'd managed to come up with a plan that enabled us to swap places for the entire summer last year, in completely different countries. Now we couldn't manage to be in two places in the same city?

Unless…

Suddenly the possibility of regaining the confidence I'd found when I pretended to be Willa felt like it was right there, waiting for me to grab it. So I did.

"We could swap places again." I said it quickly, before I lost my nerve.

Willa's face lit up. "You mean, you'd volunteer at the Shore Thing while I worked on the film?"

"Well, I was thinking the other way around," I joked. "But sure, why not?" I was still reading the Shore Thing Project website, drawn in by the stunning marine photography, and the details of all the work they did. I had to admit, it did seem genuinely amazing.

"That could work." Willa had her plotting face on now. I tried to imagine actually doing it. Walking into an office I'd never been to before and telling everyone I was Willa. Last summer, Luca and his foster mother, Willa's Aunt Sofia, had never met Willa, so they just believed I was her when I told them so. The same could happen here.

Suddenly, I spotted the massive flaw in my plan.

"Except your mum is taking us *both* to the Shore Thing Project tomorrow to meet everyone. I can't pretend to be you to people who actually know you." Willa and I look alike, but not *that* alike.

Willa scowled. "Maybe we could get out of the visit tomorrow?" she suggested. "Or... Hang on," she said.

Jumping up off the bed, Willa bounded across the room – her bedroom was about three times the size of mine at home – and opened her wardrobe, pulling out clothes until she had a complete outfit, hung on one hanger. Then she hauled my suitcase from the floor on to my bed and opened it, yanking out items of clothing and muttering to herself the whole time. "What happened to that red top I bought you?" she asked.

"It's at home." Still unworn. "What do my clothes have to do with your plan?"

"Everything!" Willa replied unhelpfully.

Finally she hung up my denim shorts, a white T-shirt with cherries printed on it and a red hoodie next to her own outfit, slinging my white Converse to the floor below. Hanging next to the pink and orange playsuit, white denim jacket and sparkly flip-flops she'd put out for herself, my clothes looked as boring as they always did compared to Willa's.

"So we have clothes," I said, looking between the outfits and Willa's beaming smile. "I still don't understand exactly how this helps."

"Which one is mine?" Willa asked, and I pointed automatically to the playsuit. "Exactly. And whoever is wearing that outfit is, of course, Willa Andrews, right?"

"But, Willa, it's so different this time. People know there are two of us, they'll be watching out for this sort of thing. Your *mum* is here, and she knows what we both look like."

"You don't have to fool my mum, that's the point." Willa sat back down on the bed beside me. "Look, here's the thing. Have you tried to spot the moment in a movie when the lead actor bails and the stunt guy takes over?"

"No."

"Well, I have. And you can't. Nearly all of the time the switch is too seamless to notice. And the stand-in is made up to look like the famous actor – same hair, same make-up, same height. But the biggest thing is—"

"They're dressed the same," I finished.

"Right! So, here's what I figure. *Obviously* we can't switch in front of Mum, she'd know instantly. But the people at the Shore Thing Project won't."

"Even after your mum has introduced us to them as ourselves, and they've seen us both together?" I shook my head. "It won't work."

"You're such a pessimist!"

"Realist," I countered.

"Look, I think it *could* work. Yes, they'll have seen us both tomorrow. But people pay a lot more attention to clothes and hairstyles and body language than they do to the slight differences in our eye colour or the fact you're a bit taller than me now. I mean, if they were going to see us together all the time then, yeah, they'd probably notice."

"But if they only see one of us … and we're dressed like and act like the other…" I filled in thoughtfully.

"People are always more likely to jump to easy conclusions," Willa said, with a shrug. "And besides, it's not like any of them will have spent a lot of time with us, or memorized our faces or anything. And *you* don't have to volunteer at the Shore Thing, so if you wander off to explore Santa Monica—"

"Or hop on a bus to go to the film set—"

"Who's going to complain?" Willa gave me a brilliant grin, and I couldn't help but return it.

"It *might* work," I admitted.

ALICE

Hey. How are things in Italy?

LUCA

The gelato is still delicious. And the donkeys miss you.

ALICE

Aw, I almost miss them too.

LUCA

More importantly, how's LA?

ALICE

Kind of amazing. Willa's house is the size of Mabel's whole block of flats.

LUCA

Wow. Bigger than the farmhouse here?

ALICE

Much bigger.

LUCA

What has my cousin got planned for your visit?

ALICE

Well. That's actually why I was messaging. I might be about to do something crazy.

LUCA

How crazy are we talking here? Is it 'stay up past midnight to watch another episode of something on Netflix' crazy or 'take a test without studying for it' crazy or 'run away and join the circus' crazy?

ALICE

I'm thinking about going along with one of Willa's plans. Except this time it was kind of MY plan.

LUCA

So we're WAY past circus, then. What is it this time? The two of you star in the movie of your summer swap, except you play Willa and she plays Alice?

ALICE

Not ... quite.

LUCA

Why do I get the feeling that this plan is a Very Bad Idea?

ALICE

Because it might be? But it might also be … kind of fun. And cool. And exactly what I need.

LUCA

So, are you going to tell me what it is?

ALICE

Actually, no. Not yet, anyway. I want to see how tomorrow goes first. If it works … well, then we have a plan. If it doesn't then we'll have to call the whole thing off anyway. So watch this space.

WILLA

Mum insisted on us all getting the bus down to Santa Monica the next day, so we knew the route.

"I probably won't be able to drive you myself most mornings, although I'll try to pick you up on the days when I'm not filming in the afternoon. But you know what my schedule is like, Willa."

"Erratic," I supplied, and she nodded. All part of the fun of working in the TV and film industry, as far as I was concerned. Who wanted a job where you were in the same place with the same things happening at the same time every day?

"It's important for you both to know how to get there safely," Mum went on as we waited for the Big Blue Bus to arrive at the stop nearest our house.

Alice nodded sagely, even though I already knew how to get to and from Santa Monica and had talked her through it last night. It was basically extra planning on top of all the planning we'd already done. Alice loved that sort of thing.

She paid attention to everything on our journey

– which tickets Mum bought, which stops we went through, where we changed buses – making notes on each detail. I tried not to get frustrated by how long it made everything take. The more comfortable Alice felt doing this journey on her own, the easier it would be for me to sneak off to filming and leave her. Not that I shared that insight with my mother.

I'd totally expected Alice to wake up nervous about the plan, even though she was the one who'd come up with it.

"Are you fretting yet?" I'd asked, ready to reassure her as soon as she sat up in bed that morning. "Because don't. We're not even going to be swapping today, because Mum will be there the whole time, right? This is just to get the lay of the land and see if the plan is going to work."

"Yeah. I know." Alice rubbed her eyes. "Actually, I don't feel that nervous. Yet."

It was that 'yet' that was worrying me. Today was the only chance I had to *really* convince Alice that the plan was viable. If anything went wrong, we'd have to bin the whole idea. We only had one shot at this.

That morning I'd presented Alice with two outfits, put together from her suitcase and my wardrobe.

"Which one is mine?" she'd asked, scrunching up her nose.

I grinned. "It doesn't matter. That's the point!"

"So … even though your whole plan is based around us wearing distinctive outfits, today we're going to dress the same?" She stared at the cropped skinny jeans, pastel vest tops and white hoodies I'd laid out.

"Because this is the real test," I explained. "It came to me last night."

Alice's eyes lit up, and I knew she'd got it. "So we see if anyone we meet today confuses us for each other, right?"

I nodded. "And if they do, we know this plan is going to work."

Mum had rolled her eyes when we'd come downstairs with our hair in the same loose plaits and our almost matching outfits. "You know I can still tell you two apart, right?"

"We know," Alice and I had chimed in unison.

But sitting on the bus, I realized that it wasn't just our clothes that gave us away. As Alice grilled Mum on everything she knew about the Shore Thing Project, and the history of LA, and how often the buses ran, and everything else under the sun, it dawned on me that it would be our personalities that gave us away, more than anything.

Alice was Alice. She seemed shy to people who didn't know her well, but when Alice was really into something – like, say, the environment – she asked *all* the questions. Which meant that *I* needed to ask questions and be interested too.

The Shore Thing Project was a short walk from the bus stop. I watched as Alice paused as we got off the bus, looking around her and memorizing her surroundings. Then she whipped her journal out of her bag and wrote down a few of the details from the bus stop. Once she was satisfied (and after Mum had made a comment about how responsible and organized Alice was, with a meaningful look in my direction) we took off towards the ocean.

I hadn't really been sure what to expect from the Shore Thing offices. As Mum led us along the Ocean Front Walk, past car parks and hotels and bike rental places, I looked out for something that looked like, maybe, a giant aquarium or something.

Instead, we arrived at a normal, boring-looking office building next to a park, just off the beach.

There was a driftwood sign out front by the beach that read 'The Shore Thing Project' and another, more professional one on the building itself, next to the front door, that had details about directors and trustees and stuff. Alice read it; I didn't.

Mum rang the doorbell and a blond woman (with excellent highlights, incidentally, just like sun streaks) opened it and threw her arms around Mum, beaming.

"Sarra! It's so good to see you! I can't believe you're living so close now and we haven't even managed a dinner since before Christmas."

"Hi, Darla." Mum hugged the woman back, then pulled away. "And thank you so much for agreeing to this. I was relieved when Principal Carter mentioned this place as a possibility! Somebody –" she shot a glare in my direction and I stood close enough to Alice that, really, she could have been furious with either of us – "got into a little trouble at school, and volunteering here this spring break was the best way out of it for all of us."

Darla flashed Alice and me a grin. "Don't worry, I understand. I have a son a few years older than you, and I've had to talk him out of trouble with Principal Carter once or twice too – usually for starting some sort of student protest over the school's environmental issues though, so it's hard to be *too* cross."

"Willa orchestrated a flash mob." Mum rolled her eyes, but I was *almost* sure there was a hint of a smile lurking around her lips. "I hate to admit it, but the resulting film is pretty amazing."

"Too right," I muttered under my breath. I'd just uploaded the final version to my channel that morning and already the hits were coming in.

Alice nudged me in the ribs, although I wasn't sure if it was to remind me not to get into any more trouble with my mum or because we weren't supposed to draw any attention to the differences between us.

"Anyway, this is Willa, and her friend Alice who is staying with us for the holiday." Mum motioned at the two of us, and we both waved back at the same time.

"Ah, the famous Alice who went along with Willa's *last* crazy plan." Darla's eyes were dancing. I got the impression that she was far more fun about things like that than Mum. "You really are very alike, aren't you?"

"Unfortunately so. Willa's the only one who is *obliged* to volunteer though, so if Alice wants to just hang out on the beach or the pier and enjoy being in California while Willa slaves away for you, that's fine by me."

I ducked my head to hide my grin. Mum was trying to push home the fact that I was being punished, but actually she'd just played straight into our plans. Now, when 'Alice' disappeared, no one would question it.

"Well!" Darla clapped her hands together. "Why don't I show you around? Or better still," she said as a tall, gorgeous surfer guy walked around the corner, "I'll let my son Jake do it, while Sarra and I have a catch-up! Jake, honey, Willa and Alice are going to be volunteering with us the next couple of weeks. Think you can give them the lowdown on what we do here?"

Jake shrugged, a lazy smile on his face, and shook his blond hair out of his eyes. "Sure thing, Mom. Welcome to the Shore Thing, guys."

Suddenly, I was regretting making other plans for spring break after all.

ALICE

Willa's mum disappeared into an office with Darla, leaving Willa and I alone with Jake. He looked about seventeen, I figured, so a couple of years older than us. He was basically what I imagined if I tried to picture a Californian teenage boy – wearing board shorts and a faded blue 'Live Life on Porpoise' T-shirt not unlike one I had in my wardrobe at home. Put a surfboard under his arm and he could have strolled straight out of one of the American TV shows I watched. He watched the mums walk away and I wondered how he felt about being lumbered with the new volunteers on a Sunday. Probably like we were 'cramping his style', as Dad would say.

"I was going to head out to the beach, but I guess I can show you two around the old place first." Jake shrugged as he said it, like he didn't really care either way. "But first, which one of you is which?"

"I'm Alice," Willa said, before I could even open my mouth. So much for 'we're just being ourselves today'.

"So you must be Willa," Jake said, and I smiled

weakly back at him. "Wait, you're the girl who set up that flash mob that dinged Mr Richards' convertible, right?"

"That's me," I said, even though it was so far away from 'me' it was laughable.

"Maybe you can help us with some new videos we need to shoot," Jake said as he started heading down the corridor into the heart of the building.

"Maybe," I said, glaring at Willa now his back was turned. Great. Now I was probably going to get stuck videoing him and his friends on their surfboards, instead of actually doing the important work I'd hoped to be involved in at the Shore Thing.

Willa made her eyes really wide, as if to say 'what was I *supposed* to do?'

I didn't dignify that with a response.

"OK, so, Mom set up the Shore Thing five years ago to focus on cleaning up the Santa Monica shoreline, and educating locals – especially school kids – about the importance of protecting our oceans." Jake sounded like he was reading from a script, although there was nothing in his hands as we walked. I guessed this was a talk he had given before, probably lots of times.

"Have you been working here with your mum the

whole time?" I asked, wondering if he *actually* got involved in the work, as well as the surfing.

"Since the start! It's been just me and Mom since I was little, so when she was setting this place up she'd bring me with her. Lucky for her I loved it, even at twelve. I mean, I love this beach, this ocean. Why wouldn't I want to help keep it clean?"

"Makes sense to me," I agreed, smiling a little. Maybe he wasn't *just* the surfer dude I'd imagined.

We stopped as the corridor opened up on to a large room.

"This is the main office here." Jake waved a hand towards a bank of desks with six or seven computers set up. "We're a non-profit organisation, but we raise enough to have five members of permanent staff, most working part-time. Mom is in charge of most of the public stuff and the fundraising. The rest of the staff coordinate school education visits, or big volunteer clean-up events, online awareness-raising, and getting involved with some of the other non-profits working on marine conservation and studies along this stretch of coast. Everything else – like dune walk clean-ups, kayak ocean sweeps, even some of the student beach walks – they're all done by volunteers. We're lucky. People care a lot about this beach, so we have a lot of help, even if some people don't hang around long when they figure out what hard work it is."

"And now you have us." I was completely rethinking my original assumptions about Jake. He really did seem to be involved in everything the Shore Thing Project was up to. I liked him a lot more because of it. "Well, me, anyway. And maybe Alice, some of the time."

I glanced over at the unusually quiet Willa. It was weird watching her play the part of, well, *me*. It was as if she'd shrunk in on herself, her shoulders hunched and her voice silenced.

I didn't look like that. Did I?

Shaking off my worries, I turned my attention back to Jake – and to being bright and bubbly Willa. If Darla talked to Mrs Andrews about what 'Willa' had been up to during her volunteer stints, we needed it to be convincing.

So. My new mantra had to be 'What Would Willa Do?' And I had no doubt that the real Willa would be scoring my performance later, once we were alone again.

"This is the staff room," Jake said, waving through an open door. "There's a fridge in there if you want to bring your own lunches, although Mom stocks some vegan snacks for everyone too." He looked both ways before leaning in closer and saying softly, "But if you're really hungry, the burger stand just down the beach is the best in town. We never eat meat at home, so it's kind of a treat. But their packaging isn't recyclable, so I try not to go *too* often."

I stifled a laugh. "I know that feeling." Trying to make the right choices for the environment *all* the time was kind of hard. "I always figure that as long as we're doing our best most of the time, that's still making a difference, right?"

"Exactly what I tell Mom!" He beamed at me. "In fact, one of the biggest issues around here right now are the electric scooters you can hire. People get so frustrated by them they're just tossing them in the ocean. There's a documentary—"

"I watched it!" I interrupted. "I couldn't believe people would do that!"

"I know, right? Wait, have you seen—"

Willa cleared her throat, trying to get Jake's attention back to the tour. "Sorry," he said. "I get kind of carried away when I'm talking about stuff that really matters to me."

"Me too," I admitted, kind of amazed to find out I actually had stuff in common with this older, cooler guy. If we'd met anywhere else, I'd have assumed he only cared about surfing and his image, and stayed far away from him.

Jake pushed open another door, ushering Willa and me inside. "Um. So, this is our education suite, which is just a fancy way of saying classroom."

Tables were laid out in a big horseshoe with enough chairs behind them to seat maybe thirty-five kids. Each table had a stack of poster paper and a pot of pens on it. There was one big window at the far end of the room that looked out over the beach and the ocean, and the other walls were covered with posters – some printed, some hand-drawn – about the importance of looking after our oceans.

"This is where we bring kids when they first arrive," Jake explained. "There's a big screen we can pull down to show them films about the work we do. Sometimes we get one of the other charities to bring in rescued sea life to show them too, which is cool."

"It sounds it," Willa said. She'd wandered over towards the window to look out over the ocean.

"It really does," I agreed, with more Willa-like enthusiasm. "So, what will I be doing the next couple of weeks?" If I was taking Willa's punishment, I hoped it would at least involve *some* fun.

Jake rattled off a few things the project had planned over spring break – mostly names of organizations running camps for kids over the holiday, or schools who only had one week off and went back the following week. I assumed they were all local and I was supposed to know about them, so just nodded along. "Oh! And there's the SOS march too, the weekend after next."

"SOS?" I asked.

"Save Our Seas," he explained. "It's an awareness march through Santa Monica, along the beach, then ending up on the deck here for a big party. Come on." Jake pushed the door and held it open for us. "I'll show you."

WILLA

The deck out the back of the Shore Thing was kind of awesome. It wrapped around three sides of the building, looking out over the beach and the ocean beyond, and had tiny fairy lights twisted around the rails. It was *perfect* for a party. Maybe I'd manage to make the party, at least, even if I was missing all the rest.

To be honest, helping out with school kids or picking up rubbish from the dunes or learning about marine life conservation – it all sounded a lot more like Alice's thing than mine. If it wasn't for the fact she would get to spend her days with the gorgeous Jake and sit out on this deck enjoying the beach during her breaks, I wouldn't have thought twice about my choice of how to spend the next two weeks.

Well, that and the grief Alice was already giving me.

"OK, so what happened to 'we'll just be ourselves today'?" she demanded, the moment our bedroom door was shut. Mum was downstairs calling out for Chinese, and the house was so big she wouldn't have heard us talking from halfway up the stairs, even if she was listening, but Alice was always over-cautious like that.

I shrugged in response. "I figured that since such a perfect opportunity presented itself we should roll with it. Improvisation, right?"

"I think I prefer a script over improv." Alice flopped on to her bed and put one arm over her eyes. And she says *I'm* dramatic.

"Look, it all went great, right?" I said, leaning over the gap between our beds. Did she even remember that this whole swap was *her* idea? "Hot Jake is absolutely sure that you're Willa, and Mum didn't notice anything when she came and got us from the deck and we all said goodbye."

"Hot Jake?" Alice lifted her arm to squint at me. "Is that what we're calling him now?"

I shrugged. "Well, isn't he?"

"I suppose." Alice probably hadn't even noticed. "I mean, I was kind of surprised. He seems really involved with the Shore Thing Project. Really believes in what they are doing there."

Yes, because activism was more attractive to Alice

than a cute face and great hair.

"And he definitely believed you were me." Hopping from my bed to hers, I sat crossed-legged beside her.

She covered her eyes again. "Because you told him you were me."

"And because you asked questions, were outgoing – even flirtatious."

That made her sit up. "I was not!"

"Well, OK, no, you weren't. But you could be!"

Alice's cheeks turned pink. "I'm pretty sure I couldn't."

"Fine. You were friendly – and that's good! You had the confidence to talk to an older boy you're going to be working with, who just happens to be gorgeous, and you didn't get embarrassed or nervous once, right?" Sometimes, I think Alice has this idea of herself as a shy, anxious loner. It's good for her to realize that that's not what *I* see.

She blinked at me, leaning back on her hands. "I *didn't*, did I? Only because I was pretending to be you though."

Personally I thought it was more likely to be because they were talking about the Shore Thing Project, and Alice cared about saving the oceans and knew loads about marine conservation because of her marine-biologist professor dad. But whatever.

If she really thought she needed to be me to bring out that side of her, well, she had the perfect opportunity ahead.

"And you get to keep doing that for the next two weeks," I pointed out.

She smiled. "Yeah. Yeah, I do."

Part of me wondered if this was the real reason Alice had suggested the swap. Did she *want* to be me again?

I remembered the text messages Hal had sent, saying that Alice had been quiet lately. Maybe even unhappy. I'd told him I'd fix it. And if hanging out with Hot Jake for two weeks didn't build her confidence, nothing would!

"The point is, we got away with it," I said. "Jake – and probably Darla – think you're Willa, and Mum didn't even notice a thing. Add in the fact that we'll switch clothes after Mum leaves tomorrow and we're golden! This is *absolutely* going to work."

Alice met my grin with her own. "I guess we'd better pick out our outfits for tomorrow, then?"

I jumped off the bed and ran to the wardrobe. "Hell yes!"

That kept us busy until Mum called us down for Chinese.

"What have you girls been doing up there?" she asked as we ladled out noodles and rice on to our plates.

"Choosing our outfits for tomorrow," I said, around a mouthful of spring roll. "We want to look good for our first day on the job!"

"Actually, you might want to pick out clothes for something else too." Mum moved the carton of spring rolls down the table, away from me. Which was mean. "I've got to do a photo shoot tomorrow night, and I thought you two might like to come along and get some shots done together too? The photographer's an old friend. I thought it might be a nice memento for Alice."

"That would be brilliant!" I'd been trying to get Mum to agree to me having professional headshots done for ages now, and this was basically the next best thing. Plus it would be cool to have a photo of me and Alice together.

Alice was frowning. "I'm not sure I really brought the right sort of clothes for a photo shoot."

I shrugged. "That's easy. You can borrow some of mine."

"It's not like you haven't done that before," Mum added.

Alice and I exchanged a quick look.

Straight after dinner, I dragged Alice back upstairs to try on more of my clothes.

"Do you do this with your other friends?" Alice asked as she shimmied into my favourite skinny jeans. "Swap clothes, I mean."

"I used to. Back home in England." I tossed her a sparkly crop top then, when she looked doubtfully at it, a black tank top to wear underneath. "I guess I've been so busy here working on my YouTube channel and doing things with Film Club, I haven't really found a new group to hang out with yet, you know?"

"Yeah, I know." Alice's voice was loaded with feeling. "Back in Cambridge I had friends."

"But not in London?"

"Nope. I mean, apart from Hal, and I'm pretty sure he's only looking after me because you asked him to." She gave me a suspicious look.

"That looks good on you." I pointed towards the mirror for her to go and see for herself. "I mean, you need make-up because of the camera lighting, and I'll do something with your hair, but I think that could definitely work."

"You think?" Alice turned from side to side as she studied her reflection.

"Definitely."

She turned to me and grinned. "Right then, your turn."

ALICE

I fell asleep visualizing the plan for the next morning and woke up panicking. I'd dreamed of the deck at the Shore Thing Project – of walking down from it, across the beach, and straight into the sea. At first, it was wonderful. But the further I walked, the more plastic and rubbish started to fill the waves around me, along with dead sea life and sea birds, until I couldn't take another step.

I sat up in bed, trying to shake off the dream, and started worrying about the plan instead. What on earth had even possessed me? But it was too late to back out now.

It was still early, according to Willa's pineapple-shaped alarm clock, so I had plenty of time to silently panic. Or, you know, work through my feelings in a more productive way. Pulling my journal from the drawer I'd stashed it in, I turned to a blank page and drew a line right down the middle. At the top of the two columns I wrote 'Awesome List' and 'Worry List'. (Other people might go with pros and cons, but this worked better for me. I was perfectly capable of worrying about some of the pros, for one thing.)

Without thinking too hard, I started writing, getting everything that was sloshing around in my head down on paper and out of my brain.

Awesome List

- Helping protect the Santa Monica shoreline, and all the creatures living there
- Learning more about actual, on the ground conservation
- Getting experience of putting together leaflets and so on
- Maybe getting to go on the awareness march?
- **Finding my confidence again by being Willa for two weeks**

Worry List

- Working at the Shore Thing Project on my own, without Willa
- Not getting to spend as much time with Willa this holiday as I'd hoped
- Screwing up somehow at the Shore Thing

- Embarrassing myself in front of Hot Jake (must stop calling him that) and the other Shore Thing volunteers
- **Getting found out**

I put down my pen and stared at my lists. Really, it all came down to the last bullet point on each of them.

If I followed the plan I could regain the confidence I'd found last summer. But if we got found out ... that would be it. I'd promised Dad I wouldn't get into any trouble this holiday. If Mrs Andrews figured out what we were doing, there was no way Willa would be allowed to visit me in London.

I looked over at Willa, still sleeping in the other bed. What would she put on her lists? Probably her Awesome List would be full of all the great things she'd be up to working on the indie movie, and her Worry List would be blank. Willa always focused on the positives and the opportunities, rather than the things that might go wrong. Maybe I should try that for a change.

What if everything went to plan for once, and at the end of the holiday I was the Alice I *wanted* to be again? I could go back to London and talk about my

LA adventures. Maybe even make some new friends. Wouldn't that be worth it?

Closing my journal, I stared over at the two outfits Willa had laid out for us.

Willa and I might have our differences but we were friends. And maybe we brought out parts of each other that wouldn't see the light of day otherwise. Because of me, Willa had spent time actually *planning* this adventure. And because of her...

I had the courage to go through with it.

"OK, so, we get in there, we say goodbye to Mum, then we dash for the bathroom," Willa whispered in my ear as we got out of Mrs Andrews' car, as if we hadn't already been through it eight times that morning. Apparently I wasn't the only one who was just a little nervous about the plan after all.

"Got it," I murmured back.

Mrs Andrews locked the car and walked us across the car park and up to the Shore Thing Project building. Unlike yesterday, the front door was wide open, letting in a sea breeze, and I could hear laughter and conversation. The knot inside my stomach tightened.

"Right, girls. You know the rules today. Do whatever Darla and her staff ask you to, don't cause any trouble, then meet me here this afternoon in time for the photo shoot. And once you're done at the Shore Thing, you're only to hang out here by the beach. OK?"

We both nodded mutely. Mrs Andrews looked suspicious, so I smiled. So did Willa.

That only made things worse. Mrs Andrews frowned and opened her mouth again, probably to give us even more specific instructions – or threats.

Luckily, at that moment Darla appeared. "Willa, Alice, you're here! Brilliant. Come on in and we'll get you set up."

"Bye, Mum." Willa kissed Mrs Andrews on the cheek.

I kept my head down. Our faces were alike enough, but there were differences if people looked closely. We needed Darla – and everyone else – to just assume that whoever was wearing bright pink and orange was Willa.

"Bye. And bye, Alice."

I waved. By the time I turned back, Willa was already halfway down the corridor, Darla just behind her.

"Actually, can I just pop to the bathroom first?" she asked, without turning round, as we passed the bathrooms Jake had pointed out on our tour the day before.

"Of course," Darla said.

"Me too," I added, ducking through the door after her.

Inside the bathroom, Willa and I stared at each other. "We're really going to do this?" I asked for the hundredth time.

Willa grinned and started getting changed. "Come on! Hand me your shorts. Then I'll do your hair."

Minutes later, we were back outside again with Darla. This time, I was Willa. Her playsuit scratched a little around the waist, and I was worried about matching the slight American twang she'd picked up over the last nine months, but it was too late to think about all that now.

I knew it would be easier once Willa was gone, and I was the only new girl here. Everyone would just assume I was Willa – because why wouldn't I be?

"Ready?"

"Let's go," I said, with my best Willa smile in place. It was showtime.

WILLA

I tried not to check my – Alice's – watch too often as Jake set us up with our first task: compiling information packs for the education days, with different ones for different age groups, more fun ones for the holiday-camp groups, and more educational ones for the school groups the following week. (I felt kind of sorry for the kids who only got one week for spring break; being used to the two-week Easter holidays back home, I'd have *definitely* complained if St Saviour's only had one week off.)

It was hard to concentrate though. The job was really boring and I knew that Matty would be there to pick me up any minute. It had taken some convincing to persuade him that it was worth swinging by the Shore Thing to pick me up at all – if I was late, I wasn't sure he'd wait for me.

This first day was going to be the hardest. Luckily Mum was filming until almost dinner time, so I'd hopefully manage to get back from the set before she arrived to collect us for the photo shoot. We'd already given her our outfits and my make-up bag, and we'd made plans to stop somewhere quick and easy for dinner on the way.

Alice, I knew, had brought a novel and her Los Angeles guidebook, and planned to hang out and explore the Santa Monica Pier once she was done with her volunteer shift. We just needed enough time to swap outfits again before Mum arrived.

"Well, this is the funnest way *ever* to spend spring break," I said, after Jake had left the room and it was just Alice and me in the education suite. Jake was definitely hot but, on the evidence so far, way too goody-goody for me. Especially if he thought these leaflets were a good time for all. I reckoned he could be *perfect* for Alice though.

I picked up the first of the leaflets, which featured a picture of a plastic bag floating on the ocean. The next showed dead fish lined up on the sand. The third had a graph showing how long it took everyday items to biodegrade (spoiler: some don't, ever).

"Hmm?" Alice looked up from where she was obviously reading every word of the leaflets with intense concentration. "Yeah, it's great, isn't it?"

There was no sarcasm in her voice. Apart from Jake, only *Alice* could think that organizing depressing leaflets about the future of the planet was a fun way to spend her holiday.

I checked my watch again. "Matty is going to be here soon, so I need to head out and meet him." That got Alice's attention. "Will you be OK here?"

Alice's smile didn't quite reach her eyes. "Sure. That's the plan, right?"

"Yeah. Look, I'll text when I'm headed back. And I'm sure Jake would be thrilled if you decided to hang out here and sort leaflets later this afternoon, if you don't want to explore Santa Monica on your own." There was a horrible feeling worming its way through my insides. I had a suspicion it might be guilt.

I shook it off. Alice had agreed to help me, after all.

"OK, so what are you going to tell Jake?" I asked.

"That 'Alice' got bored and decided to go explore the pier, since she's never been to LA before, and she doesn't want to spend her whole holiday stuck in here."

"Perfect!" She'd even managed to get in some of the eye-rolling I'd included last night when I demonstrated to her what she should say. Maybe she wasn't such a bad actress after all.

I jumped to my feet and Alice followed, giving me a quick hug. "Good luck with the film."

"And good luck with the … leaflets!" I flashed her one last smile and headed out the door.

Matty was waiting for me in a car park a couple of buildings down, just as we'd arranged.

"You ready for this?" he asked as I hopped into the passenger seat. "Remember, this is my reputation on the line. I told them you were worth taking a chance on, so you really can't let me down. Got it?"

"Hundred per cent." This was my chance to see how a film actually came together. And I just knew that my behind-the-scenes documentary would be a huge hit on my channel. "Everyone agreed to me filming them, right?"

Matty nodded as he pulled out into the sluggish LA traffic. I could never get over how long it took to get *anywhere* in this city. But at least the view out over the ocean was pretty while we were crawling along.

"Fran liked your flash mob video edit. She said she's happy for you to film – that it might even be nice to have a record of the shoot—"

"Great!"

"*But*," Matty went on, "the deal is that you can't let it interfere with everything else we need you to do as production assistant, OK? We're working a skeleton crew on this one; that's the only reason I could get you on the team. The rest of the class already filmed their – totally derivative – project before the break."

"I heard." I'd tried to get involved with that one too but had no luck.

"So everybody really has to pull their weight. You got it?"

"I got it," I promised solemnly. Just as long as no one expected me to waste time on stuff that didn't matter, when I had my *own* film to make. Jenn was there for that stuff, right?

By the time we arrived at the park, halfway between Santa Monica and home, the others were already there. Matty's stride lengthened when he spotted them, and I scurried a little to catch up.

"Matty! You made it. We were starting to wonder about you." A girl with a mass of black curls shoved her phone in the back pocket of her skinny jeans and gave him a hug. I recognized her instantly – Fran Levine, our director. I felt my heart speed up a bit in anticipation of actually *working* with her.

"Sorry, Fran. Traffic was a beast. I had to collect your production assistant from Santa Monica beach."

Fran turned to me, one perfectly sculpted eyebrow

raised. She wore a loose tank top with a faded slogan on it over another, tighter black tank – a simple, casual look that, on her, somehow had the appearance of something off a catwalk. "So, you're the girl who flash-mobbed the exams, huh?"

"Willa." I stuck a hand out for her to shake and hoped it wasn't too sweaty. "Thanks for letting me on the team. I love the short film you did about the—"

Her palm was smooth and cool in mine. "Just try and keep up, yeah? And when I say jump—"

"I ask 'how high?'" I finished confidently. I totally had this.

Fran's eyebrow inched a little closer to her hair. "You jump," she corrected. "We don't have time to waste on questions. We've got a film to make. Jenn!"

Spinning abruptly on her heel, she gestured at Matty's girlfriend, who came hurrying over. "Can you show Willa around, introduce her to everyone? Matty, Tyler is already setting up the equipment over where we'll be filming." Matty was halfway across the park before she finished speaking. Apparently, you didn't hang around when Fran asked you to do something.

"Come on, then," Jenn said with a distinct lack of enthusiasm.

It didn't matter. I had enough for both of us. As we weaved through the park I saw two seniors I recognized having their hair and make-up styled by another, plus Matty and Tyler setting up half the school's camera and lighting equipment. Another guy and a girl, sitting in the sort of director's chairs I'd seen on real film sets, had their heads bent over a script, presumably discussing the scene we were about to film.

"That's Finn and Kat," Jenn said, waving a hand at the pair, "our stars. The two in hair and make-up are Polly and Bethany – and the guy doing the make-up is Derek. He's in charge of costumes too." I waved at them all. Only Derek waved back, sending powder flying from his brush.

Jenn stopped beside a wheeled metal cart, painted bright turquoise. "This here is the props cart. It's my responsibility, but if anything goes missing from it I'll be blaming you."

I blinked but Jenn was already moving on. "Wait – what?" I asked, chasing after her. She ignored me.

"Matty is our director of photography and location scout," she said, ticking her boyfriend's roles off on her fingers. "Tyler's the gaffer – that means he's in charge of lighting."

"I know what a gaffer is," I said irritably.

"He's also basically our grip. Lara's in charge of sound," she added as we passed a girl with large headphones on, who ignored us. "And Fran is our beloved leader. Or director, as we call it."

"And you're a production assistant like me," I said, smiling sweetly as I reminded her that she wasn't *actually* above me on this project.

"PA *and* props *and* camera assistant," Jenn said defensively. I figured the last one was probably only because she was dating the director of photography. Although I could now totally understand the rumour about her only being there to keep an eye on Matty and Fran. Fran was loads cooler than Jenn any day.

"Jenn! We need those coffees now!" Fran yelled, and Jenn bustled off towards a coffee cart on the edge of the park.

I turned my attention back to the real action. While Jenn had given me the tour, the others had been setting up their first scene. Matty had his camera ready and Lara gave a nod that the sound was right. Finn and Kat were already in position in front of the park's only fountain. I felt a shiver go through me as everyone went silent, waiting.

Then Fran called, "Action."

And in that moment, I knew I was exactly where I was meant to be.

ALICE

"Did we lose Alice already?" Jake asked, when he slipped back into the education suite to help me with the leaflets. "I kind of got the impression she wasn't thrilled about spending her holiday here."

I forced a smile. "Well, I guess it's probably not what she imagined doing." It felt so weird talking about myself in the third person. Weirder even than sitting there in Willa's clothes, talking to Jake as if I talked to cute, older guys all the time.

The last time I'd tried to impress a cute, older guy it had gone badly. Jake didn't seem much like Antonio, who I'd had such an excruciating crush on last summer. And, as cute as Jake was, I didn't experience the twisting in the stomach or the uncontrollable blushing, and my heart was even maintaining its normal tempo. Definitely a win.

I liked Jake though. I liked how much he cared about the Shore Thing Project and how laid back he seemed to be about everything else. I hoped we could become friends.

"It's a shame. I mean, I know you *have* to be here, but it's always nice when we win someone new over to the cause. I guess I didn't impress Alice much with the tour yesterday."

I knew that, actually, Jake had impressed Willa plenty – she just had bigger priorities. But I couldn't tell him that.

"Alice isn't always great at committing to things that aren't, well, her main interests." Urgh. I hated saying that about myself, even if I was actually talking about Willa. I hated making myself sound like a flake when actually, I was the one there doing the work! And I felt doubly guilty because Willa *was* committed – just not to the Shore Thing Project.

"Activism isn't for everybody," Jake said with a shrug. "I mean, people say they care about the planet, about the environment, the oceans, the rainforests, whatever. But words don't really go very far. It's when people are willing to actually do something about it that change happens."

"Like we were saying yesterday, it's about lots of people making small changes, rather than a few people doing everything perfectly." I liked that idea a lot. I liked knowing that small changes could build and build into bigger ones – that I didn't have to be perfect all the time, I just had to keep trying. With environmental activism *and* life. "Things like cutting out single-use plastics," I carried on, thinking about how Mabel had started shopping at a place that let her refill her own containers, rather than buying new ones every time.

"Exactly!" Jake looked pleased. "None of us are perfect, but at least we're trying. Hey, we're actually going to be doing a new presentation for the education suite about single-use plastics, for the next semester of school trips. Maybe you could help, if you wanted?"

"I'd like that." Willa wouldn't have, I knew, but Willa wasn't here. I was.

"Great! Now why don't I show you what the Shore Thing is really all about?"

I was excited to see what Jake had planned for me next – and when he swung past his mum's office to tell her we were headed out, I was even more curious.

"OK, so I know you've been living in Los Angeles for a while now, but have you spent much time here at Santa Monica beach?" Jake asked as he opened the gate on the deck and led me down to the sand. Just the feel of it under my trainers, slipping and sinking, made me feel better.

"Not nearly as much as I should have," I answered honestly.

The seaside is my happy place, always has been.

"Then let me show you around," Jake said with a grin. "Do you want to give Alice a call, see if she wants to join us?"

"Um, sure." I faked a smile and fished in my pocket for my phone. Angling it so he couldn't see the screen, I pretended to call Willa, then held the phone to my ear.

"Voicemail," I mouthed to Jake. Then, talking into the phone, I said, "Hi, Alice. Just checking in. Jake and I are going to walk along the beach a bit before Mum comes to pick us up. If you get this in time, call me back and we'll see if we can find you."

Heart pounding, I shoved my phone back in the pocket of my playsuit. "Her phone is rubbish for signal here," I lied. "Let's go."

The Shore Thing offices were on the south end of Santa Monica beach. I knew from my guidebook that the whole beach was about three and a half miles long, so walking the length of it would take a while. I was just happy to be there with the sun on my shoulders and the sound of the waves lapping against the sand.

"This end of the beach is the closest to the city," Jake

explained as we walked. "You can walk straight off the street on to the beach – and people do."

"I can tell." Looking around, I could see the sands were packed with people with towels and swimming costumes and bodyboards – but also with joggers, walkers, and a guy in a suit talking on his mobile.

"There's a bike track that runs twenty-two miles along this coastline," Jake said, pointing towards a trail where two cyclists were just approaching. "And up here by the pier is the famous Muscle Beach."

My eyes widened at the sight of so many people working out, right there on the beach. It was hard to imagine that kind of gym on the sand at Hunstanton.

We bypassed the famous Santa Monica Pier I'd read about in my guidebook – and where I'd intended to spend my afternoon, waiting for Willa. I looked across at the Ferris wheel and the rollercoaster, outlined against the bright blue sky. I could hear shrieks and laughter and music, and wondered for a moment if I should suggest we stop. The real Willa would have, I knew. But Jake didn't suggest it, and besides, he was showing me the beach, not the pier.

Instead Jake kept walking up along the north side of the beach. In some parts, we kept to the Ocean Front Walk, in others we walked along the sand.

I kicked off my shoes and socks and carried them as we walked, enjoying the hot sand against the soles of my feet and between my toes.

The further we walked, the further away from the city I felt. On the south beach, you were only a step away from the hustle and bustle of Santa Monica's streets. On the north, a bluff called the Palisades rose at the edge of the sand, separating us from the city. Of course, there was still a fairly major highway between us but, well, this was LA. Even I knew that the car was king here.

I alternated between looking up at the palm trees, at the hotels and cars zooming past, and out to sea. Every so often we'd pass a pale blue-green lifeguard station, with a bright yellow and red van beside it.

"I kind of feel like I'm in a TV show, being here," I admitted.

Jake laughed. "I know what you mean. Sometimes they film stuff down here, but mostly TV crews stick to less crowded beaches for filming."

"Makes sense." We walked a little further. "So, I read in one of the leaflets this morning that the water around Santa Monica Pier is ... not great."

Jake winced. "Understatement." Leaning over, he scooped up a plastic sandwich wrapper from the sand

and tossed it in the next bin we passed. "And the beach itself… I don't understand how people can just dump this stuff."

"Me neither."

"I mean, some things that I know are good for the environment are harder to do – or to give up."

"Like burgers from your favourite stall?"

"And taking planes on holiday or driving a car in LA," he said with a nod. "But the easy stuff? Like putting trash in the garbage can or taking your own coffee cup to a Starbucks? I don't get why we can't all do that."

"I guess I came here on a plane – I mean, back when we moved here," I added hurriedly. I'd been chatting with Jake so easily about things that mattered to me, that I'd almost forgotten I was supposed to be Willa. "But maybe working at the Shore Thing can even out my karmic balance, right?"

"I reckon so." Jake glanced sideways at me. "I know you're only supposed to be working a few hours a day, but we've got a beach clean-up planned on Wednesday evening, if you wanted to help out?"

I smiled up at him. I had no idea what Willa had planned for Wednesday but this was something that mattered.

"I'd love to."

WILLA

The weirdest thing about working on the project – a film called *Now and Then* – was not being in charge. Of anything.

So far, most of my filming experience had been solo, or with me playing director as well as shooting it alongside someone else, like Matty. Here, I just had to do as I was told.

Which, as everyone who knows me knows, is not my strong point.

Still, I was more than willing to give it a go for the experience of working with Fran Levine.

Working with others meant there were, obviously, a lot more people around. Which was great for me, as it meant I had more people to chat with about their roles in the film – preferably on camera so I could use it for my documentary.

But for my first day, the person I wanted to shadow most was Fran.

She was hard to keep up with; she never stopped moving, she seemed to be everywhere at once and nothing escaped her attention. One moment she was behind the camera with Matty, checking the framing of a shot, the next she was talking with Finn and Kat about how they should play the scene, or changing their blocking, then she was checking a costume detail with Derek. I chased after her, taking notes on everything she said, however unimportant.

By the time I'd been on set an hour, I knew one thing for certain – by the time *I* was a senior, I wanted to be Fran Levine.

She just oozed confidence and competency. People listened to her and did exactly what she asked because they knew she was good at her job. I wanted that too.

"OK, let's take that scene from the top," Fran said, clapping her hands, and everyone scurried to be in the right place.

"You're supposed to be helping me, you realize," Jenn muttered as she rushed past to move some props.

"I'm assisting the director," I replied confidently. "I'm sure she'd tell me if she wanted me to be doing something else."

"Willa! Clear those coffee cups!" Fran yelled, and I ran to obey.

Don't ask how high, just do it. That was the rule.

I shifted the last of the detritus – disposable cups.

Alice wouldn't approve, I thought, as I shoved them in the nearest bin.

"Scene ten, take three," Jenn said, and snapped the clapperboard together before stepping out of shot.

Finn and Kat gave it a moment, then began the scene, saying the lines that would become *very* familiar to all of us on set before the end of the day.

"I saw you across the park, so engrossed in your book," Finn said, in character. "And I had to come and ask what you were reading."

"It's a book of my grandmother's," Kat replied, holding up the cover to show him. "*Home from Eden* by Bea-Beatrice— Sorry, Beatrix—"

"Cut!" Fran yelled. "Reset."

And so we started again.

In between takes, while Fran got Kat to say the words 'Beatrix Frost' over and over again, I checked the shot list for the day. With any film, it's rare to shoot the scenes in the actual order they appear in the script. Fran and her team had set the schedule to make the most of our filming days at different locations. We were at the park today, then at the school for a few days, and then down in Santa Monica for the last week of filming. Which meant we only had today to shoot all the scenes set in the park – and if Kat couldn't get the lines right, that might take a while.

The shot schedule was challenging. But still…

I stood back for a second and let it all soak in. Here I was, in a park in LA, surrounded by crowded roads and palm trees, the hustle and bustle of the city moving around me. Skyscrapers loomed overhead and parched grass crunched underfoot, the Californian sun shining down on all of it.

And I was making a movie.

I grinned, even as Fran called to reset the scene for the fifth time.

By the time we finally wrapped for the day, I knew I was cutting it close to get back to the Shore Thing Project before Mum picked us up for the photo shoot. I hopped impatiently from foot to foot, waiting for Matty and Jenn to finish packing up his cameras, then bounced impatiently in the backseat of the car all the way back to Santa Monica…

Only to find that Alice wasn't there. And neither was Jake.

"Sorry, Alice, I think Willa and Jake went for a walk on the beach," Darla said with a sympathetic smile. "I'm sure they'll be back soon."

Great. So now I was being third-wheeled by *myself.*

I paced the deck, waiting for them to return, Alice's red hoodie wrapped around me. If Mum got here before Alice and I had a chance to swap our clothes back, she'd know for *sure* that there was something going on. What was Alice playing at?

Finally I spotted them approaching along the beach, ice creams in their hands. I knew the moment Alice spotted me, because she quickly spun round to say something to Jake then shoved the rest of her ice cream in her mouth and sprinted towards the deck.

"Is she here yet?" she asked breathlessly.

"Not yet," I said, annoyance leaking out in my tone. "Come on."

I dragged her towards the bathrooms and we got changed, racing out front to meet Mum just as her car pulled into the car park.

I wanted to ask Alice where she'd been, what she'd been thinking, but I couldn't – not with Mum there. Still, since we had to pretend we'd both been there the whole time, I pretty much got to hear all about Alice's long, romantic walk on the beach with Hot Jake. (She claimed they were talking about littering and sea pollution, but they were eating ice cream and laughing when *I* saw them.) I embellished the walk part of her story with some stuff I'd done last time I was down at the beach with friends, visiting Santa Monica Pier, so it at least sounded like I'd been there too.

"Oh, and there's a beach clean-up planned on Wednesday evening too," Alice added when I finished. "Jake mentioned it... I'd quite like to help out, if that's OK?" I widened my eyes at her in a 'what beach clean-up?' way. Surely part of the plan was that we talked about these things first? But it was too late now. Mum already thought it was a *brilliant* idea.

"We can *all* help out!" she said, beaming. "It'll be so great to spend some time with both you girls, doing something that really matters. And I finish shooting early on Wednesday anyway, so I can just meet you there!"

"Great!" I said, trying to sound enthusiastic.

I obviously succeeded. "So your stint as a volunteer isn't going too badly so far, then?" Mum asked. "It's nice to see you both so enthusiastic about something."

"Could be worse," I said with a shrug. "Sorting leaflets wasn't exactly a blast, but you know how I like the pier."

"Trust you to find a way to have fun even when

you're being punished," Mum said. But she was smiling, so I don't think she minded too much. "Come on, let's grab some dinner then get glammed up for our photos!"

ALICE

I could tell that Willa was annoyed about me being late to meet her, and about agreeing to the beach clean-up without talking to her first, but there wasn't anything I could do about it until we were alone again. And she seemed to cheer up at the prospect of having our photos taken, anyway.

We grabbed burgers and fries at a drive-through diner, then drove through the city to the photographer's studio.

"Jacinta is lovely," Willa's mum said as we sat in traffic. "She makes you feel really comfortable when she's shooting you. I think you're both going to really enjoy it."

As a person who generally hides when anyone gets a camera out, I was less sure. But I was trying to step out of my comfort zone here in LA, so I was willing to give it a try.

Jacinta met us at the door, hugging Mrs Andrews and Willa, and giving me a huge smile before deciding to hug me too.

"My word, you two really *do* look alike, don't you?" she said as she ushered us inside.

I hid a smile. Was there *anyone* Mrs Andrews hadn't told about our summer swap last year? As angry as she'd been at the time, it was obviously a story she loved to tell. I reckoned she was secretly even a little bit proud of Willa for pulling it off.

Willa and I were shown into a changing area, while Jacinta helped Mrs Andrews choose her own clothes before handing her over to the make-up artist.

"Right, let's get you looking all shiny!" Willa said, gleefully pulling clothes from the bag her mum had left us.

I changed into the skinny jeans, vest top and sparkly crop top we'd picked out the night before. They'd looked good in Willa's mirror, but now I was outside the safety of her bedroom I wasn't so sure. Were the sparkles too much?

Then I turned to see Willa in the capri pants with sequins she'd chosen, and a lacy, strappy top covered by a feathery, fluffy short cardigan, and realized my outfit was probably just right – for LA, with Willa.

"OK, you sit here and I'll do your hair and make-up." Willa guided me to a chair in front of a mirror surrounded by lights, and pulled out her make-up bag.

I tried not to tense up as she approached my face with brushes and sponges. I didn't tend to wear much make-up at all and we'd agreed that for this week, wearing minimal make-up would work best for both of us. But now Willa was clearly going all out.

"So," she said as she brushed powder over my forehead. "Beach clean-up?"

I winced. I'd known she'd have something to say about that. "Sorry. But it's important! And I didn't think your mum would decide we should all do it together."

She waved away my apology with her make-up brush. "It'll be fine. I'll just have to make sure I'm back well before she gets there. We can wear similar outfits that day instead of switching – and keep Mum far enough away that she doesn't hear Jake calling you Willa."

"Yeah, that's … a good idea." I wondered if Willa could tell that I hadn't really thought about that part. Which wasn't like me. I frowned. I couldn't let myself get distracted like that. "Anyway. How was filming?"

"How was Hot Jake?" Willa countered, raising her eyebrows in the lit-up mirror.

"I told you and your mum everything about today over dinner. I want to hear about the movie."

"I'm not sure you can really call it a movie," she admitted. "It's just a short film. But it was so cool to see how it all came together, all the different jobs that people have to do. I mean, I've read about it, watched YouTube 'making of' videos and that kind of thing. I've even roped in a friend or two to help me out with my films a few times. This project, though… I know it's just a student movie, and a low-budget one at that. But it felt like the real thing, you know?"

I smiled at her in the mirror as she approached my face with a mascara wand. "It sounds brilliant! So, tell me about all the people you're working with."

She gave me a basic rundown of the cast and crew, but mostly she seemed to want to fan-girl about Fran and moan about Jenn. And she had a lot to moan about there, it seemed.

"I guess she's just trying to do the best job she can," I said, when Willa told me about the prop trolley thing, but I knew I sounded doubtful. "Or maybe she was joking. I mean, how can it be *your* fault if something goes missing when she already said the prop trolley was *her* responsibility?"

"She wasn't joking," Willa said darkly, swiping at my eyelashes a little too furiously. "She doesn't want me there. But that's OK, because I don't want her there either." She sounded a little brighter at that.

I laughed. "How about your behind-the-scenes documentary? Did you get any good footage for that?"

"No." Willa sighed. "I was so busy running around moving things or holding a light that I didn't have a moment to film *anything*."

"Tomorrow will be better, I'm sure," I said.

"I thought I was the optimist of this partnership?"

I shrugged. "I've been being you all day. I guess some of it stuck."

"Are you girls ready?" The door opened, and Jacinta stuck her head round it. "Because I can't wait to photograph you both!"

I wasn't really sure what to expect from a proper photo shoot – the only photos I'd ever really sat for before were school ones. Jacinta led us into the studio and I smiled to see the hot-pink velvet sofa, and the boxes of fun hats and glasses and signs.

"OK, so I thought we'd have some fun and loosen up first, right?" Jacinta grabbed her camera and motioned towards the boxes. "So just have a play and relax."

Willa gave a *whoop* and started pulling things out of the boxes, handing some of them to me. I held up an oversized pair of sunglasses to my face and laughed, as Willa put on a pink feather boa and a straw hat.

Music burst out of the speakers and before I really knew what was happening, Willa and I were up on the sofa, dancing and singing along. I didn't even realize that Jacinta was already taking photos of us until Willa made me turn to the camera and pull a face with her.

Who knew having your photo taken could be so much fun?

We took a few more normal, posed shots of us sitting on the sofa together, but by that point we were laughing so hard, I couldn't imagine how they'd come out. Mrs Andrews came back in at that point and rolled her eyes at our antics, but she was laughing too.

"Thanks, girls," Jacinta said as we finished up. "That was the most fun photo shoot I've had in ages. I'll email you some of my favourites in the next couple of days, OK?"

"Thanks!" we chorused.

I'd expected we'd get changed again before heading home but instead we walked out in our photo outfits. And I realized, to my surprise, that I didn't even feel uncomfortable.

LA was working its magic, just like I'd hoped.

WILLA

The next morning went much as the one before. After this, Mum's call schedule meant she wasn't even going to be taking us to the Shore Thing Project for the next few days, leaving us to catch the bus, so I told Alice we didn't need to bother swapping clothes *every* day.

"I think we should." Alice glanced nervously towards the building. "Just in case."

"In case of what?" I asked.

"Oh, you know. Just in case."

Which wasn't any kind of an answer at all, but since Matty would be there any minute I went along with the swap anyway. At least the cropped jeans and tank I'd chosen for Alice looked a bit like something Fran or one of the others on set would wear. Maybe it would help me fit in more.

We were filming at the school today, which meant I had the lay of the land. Still, it was kind of weird being there when no one else was. The film teacher, Mr Harris, had given Fran the key for the equipment cupboard before the break, so we had access to even more than just the stuff they'd brought to the park the day before. I was jangling with excitement at the idea of getting my hands on it, even though I knew that, realistically, I'd probably be doing more of the moving scenery and fetching coffee side of things. Still, I could ask the others lots of questions about the tech when I interviewed them for my behind-the-scenes documentary.

The film Fran and the others were making was a sort-of love story, sort-of time-travel story. It was half about a couple in 2020, played by Finn and Kat, and half about a couple from the year the school was built, back in the eighties, who were played by Polly and Bethany. The action switched between the two time frames but used the same locations. We had to be super careful not to let anything from 2020 slip on to set when it was supposed to be 1988 or whatever, so Jenn and I spent a lot of time moving items out of shot.

"They couldn't have just picked a story that all took place in the modern era?" I asked under my breath, as Tyler helped me shift a computer desk and replace it with a vintage Apple computer he'd found in his parents' attic.

"Fran wanted to tell a story with layers," he replied.

"Modern layers would have been good," I muttered.

Still, once we were all set up, things were actually going pretty well. Derek was having a field day with the 1980s outfits and Polly and Bethany looked fab.

"Too much?" he asked as he spun Polly's chair around from the mirror propped up in the corner of our makeshift changing room (an English classroom) to face me.

I took in the electric-blue eyeshadow and crimped hair with a critical eye, then shrugged. "It's the eighties. There was no such thing as too much." I knew my fashion history, even if my *actual* history grades weren't quite so good.

Polly beamed and jumped out of the chair to find her leg warmers, while Bethany took her place for her own transformation from normal teenager to retro heroine.

"Willa! Come look at this." Matty called me over to where he was setting out camera equipment on a long row of desks. I rushed over to coo appreciatively.

I did manage to get a little filming done for my behind-the-scenes project though, using my own trusty Canon camera that I'd guilted my dad into buying me for Christmas. Capturing how Derek transformed Bethany into a perfect 1980s teenager and some great footage of Fran giving notes to Polly meant at least I was getting somewhere. In fact, I was so engrossed in filming the filming, I almost missed the moment that the classroom door opened and Principal Carter walked in.

Heart racing, I dropped instantly to the floor, under the nearest desk. Why hadn't I thought of this? We were at school! Of course there was a chance he might show up, even during the holidays. And if he saw me here, there was no chance of *him* mistaking me for Alice.

Lucky for me, he seemed engrossed in the action, standing with his arms folded across his chest and a faint smile on his face. Once I was sure he hadn't seen me, I started inching forwards under the desks, towards the door that connected this classroom with the neighbouring one. We were using that room as our hair, make-up and costume department, so the door was still open.

My face hot and my breath sounding too loud in my ears, I crawled through the desk tunnel, every second expecting someone to call out and ask me what I was doing. But they didn't. For the first time I was grateful that I was so unimportant on this shoot. At least it meant that no one missed me.

Finally, I reached the end of the tables, a metre or two away from door. Glancing back, I saw that Principal Carter was still focused on Bethany and Polly's scene. I'd have to chance it. Fists clenched so tight my nails dug into my palms, I ducked out from the table and through the half open door in one fluid, perfectly timed movement.

Then I hid behind the door, leaning against the wall, and blew out a long, long breath.

That was *too* close.

The door crashed into me as someone pushed it fully open, long before my heart rate had returned to normal.

"What are you doing slacking off in here?" Jenn asked, scowling at me. She shut the door so our conversation wouldn't disturb the filming. "Fran needs us to set up for the next scene."

I scoured my memory for the sequence of the shot list, trying to remember where the next scene was being filmed. "The quad! Perfect, let's go."

I moved to the classroom door, grateful for an excuse to escape – only for it not to budge when I tried the handle.

"That one's locked," Jenn said offhandedly. "We have to go back through this way. Come on."

She opened the adjoining door back to the classroom where the others were filming, and I flinched in case Principal Carter spotted me through the open door.

"Are you coming, or what?" she hissed at me.

"Is the principal still there?"

Jenn's eyebrows jumped up. "Why does that matter?"

I gave what I hoped was an expressive shrug and she rolled her eyes. With a sigh, she checked through the door, just as Fran yelled, "Cut!" again.

"No, he's gone," Jenn said. "Now come on!"

"Coming!" I sang, and raced past her, hoping that Principal Carter's office didn't look out over the quad. I was going to have to be careful to keep to the shadows today.

ALICE

Wednesday, Willa's mum had an early-ish call on set, so we agreed we'd catch the bus to Santa Monica and the Shore Thing Project.

"We can go in later today," Willa explained. "Since we'll be there all evening for the clean-up anyway."

"Just make sure you text to let me know you've got there safely," Mrs Andrews said. We promised we would.

"Like I *always* do," Willa added.

Of course, what this *really* meant was that I had to navigate the bus system by myself for the first time, while Willa skipped off to filming. "Next week we'll be filming some days on the beach," she said as she walked me to the bus stop. "So that'll make things easier."

"Great." What I really wanted to say was, *I can't do this on my own! What if I get lost? I don't know this city at all!*

But Willa wouldn't say those things, and I was being Willa this week. So instead I just said, "I'll see you this afternoon, then."

I was glad I'd taken notes in my journal and downloaded the LA public transport apps to my phone. Being well-prepared made me feel more confident about making the journey alone. And once I was on the bus, I realized it wasn't all that much different from finding my way around London. Well, except for the palm trees and the sunshine.

Jake and I spent the afternoon preparing for the beach clean-up – making sure we had enough reusable bags, gloves, water bottles and so on, and posting reminders on social media to try to get a good turnout. Jake had friends coming, and he seemed pleased that Mrs Andrews and 'Alice' would be joining us too.

It wasn't until we were waiting on the deck for the first of our clean-up volunteers to arrive that Jake turned to me and said, "Hey, have you ever been out in a kayak?"

I bit my lip. I knew that it wasn't exactly the sort of thing that Willa would normally do, but I wasn't being Willa tonight, was I? She'd be there to be herself. Even if Jake didn't know that. And *Alice* loved kayaking. I'd been with my dad loads of times – we'd even done a harbour clean-up in kayaks once on holiday.

"I have, actually. Not for a while now, but … I really like kayaking."

A broad smile spread across Jake's face. "Great! The Project has a few special kayaks – made out of the plastic waste we've collected from the ocean."

"That's brilliant!"

"Yeah. It was kind of my idea. Mom helped me find someone who'd be able to make them for us. They grind up all the plastic into this black powder, then pour it into these moulds… Anyway, it's pretty cool. And they're what me and my friends use for these clean-ups. We've got a spare tonight, if you want it?"

"Definitely!"

It was only after I agreed that I realized I hadn't spoken to Willa about the idea.

Willa only arrived ten minutes before her mum, but that was long enough for me to explain the slight change of plan to her.

It didn't go as well as I'd hoped.

"Wait, so you're going to be off riding the ocean waves with Hot Jake, while I pick up other people's trash on the sand dunes with my *mother*?"

"Look at it this way; if I'm out there with Jake, your

mum won't hear him call me Willa." I didn't remind her that this plan was all for her benefit in the first place. I was pretty sure she was remembering – and regretting – that anyway. "Besides, I'll be picking up other people's rubbish too. Just from a kayak."

I couldn't help the grin that spread across my face. I was so looking forward to being out on the water again.

Willa scowled at me. "You really didn't plan this?"

"I swear, Jake didn't even mention the kayaks until a couple of hours ago."

Sighing, she slouched to lean against the railings, just as I spotted Mrs Andrews approaching from the car park. "Fine. I guess you're right. It'll help with the plan."

"Exactly!" I gave her a swift hug, waved to Mrs Andrews, then headed out to find Jake before he came to find me and called me the wrong name.

It didn't take long to get Jake's friends together and loaded up with their kayaks, paddles, and rubbish-collecting kit. One or two wore short wetsuits, but the weather was still so warm I stuck with my one-piece swimsuit under my denim shorts and turquoise T-shirt that almost matched Willa's.

Jake, meanwhile, was wearing a full-length wetsuit

despite the heat, and getting ribbed for it by his friends.

"Jake *always* wears the full suit," one of them told me, leaning close with a smirk. "It's because he's scared of the terrifying jellyfish, lurking out there in the waves."

I turned to Jake to find out if it was true, and he shrugged.

"I got stung once," he said shortly. "Don't want it to happen again. Now, come on. We've got work to do out there!"

Wearing a borrowed pair of beach shoes, I copied Jake as he pushed his kayak out into the waves, then jumped in as soon as the water was deep enough. I knew I'd get wet, but that was OK. I'd brought a change of clothes anyway. And the moment the sea breeze hit my face, I knew I wouldn't care if I got soaked to the skin and had to travel back on the bus that way.

I was at sea, and I was at peace.

Us kayakers stuck together, only spreading out enough to tackle different pockets of rubbish, blown together by the tide. It was amazing how much waste there was hiding between the waves.

"It looks so beautiful and clear from the beach,"

I said as Jake bobbed past me, his rubbish bag almost full.

"Just like the whole planet looks green and blue from space," he replied, fishing out another metal drinks can and adding it to his bag. "That's why we need people to pay more attention."

"Like with your awareness march." I remembered him saying something about it on my first day. "Weekend after next, right?"

"Right." He flashed me a smile, like he was pleased I'd remembered. "You'll be there?"

I grinned back. "Wouldn't miss it." Then I paddled off towards a couple of floating bottles I'd spotted.

The sun was slowly starting its evening descent by the time we headed back to shore as a pack, our bags full. My face stung from sunshine and sea spray, and I had a feeling I should have put more sun cream on my shoulders. My hair was stiff with salt, my muscles ached from the paddling and I couldn't remember the last time I felt so alive.

So Alice.

WILLA

I'm not sure this is entirely going to plan.

HAL

One of YOUR plans? Going awry? I can't believe it.

WILLA

A little support here, please?

HAL

Fine, what's the problem?

WILLA

I think Alice is having more fun than I am.

WILLA

Thanks to Principal Carter's untimely interruption the day before, I hadn't had a chance to film much more for my documentary – I'd been too busy hiding in the shadows. Which was just fine, because I'd also been too busy picking up crisp packets and soda cans on the beach while Alice frolicked in the waves with Jake to catch up with editing the footage I *did* have.

OK, I'll admit it. I was not in my best mood ever when I headed to the school for another day of filming the next morning.

But I did have a plan.

I was on this project for more than my ability to shift tables and stand still long enough for Tyler to set the lighting. Matty had vouched for me because he believed in my talent. And if Fran wasn't going to use my creative vision or filming knowhow, then *I* would. Which meant I didn't have time for all the dogsbody jobs they kept sending my way.

But Jenn did. That was why she was there, right? As far as I knew she'd never even taken a film class and she wasn't a senior either. She could do all the grunt work, and I could get on with my behind-the-scenes film.

"Finn, do you have a sec?" I asked as he sat re-reading the script in the corner of the classroom.

He looked up and smiled his film-star smile – I reckoned he'd been practising that one in the mirror. "Sure."

I held up my camera. "I'd love to get your thoughts on the film…"

Finn, it turned out, was more than happy to talk on camera – mostly about himself. Kat gave me a bit more background about how the film came about though, which was interesting.

"Normally the Senior Class just works on one big project together for the end of year showcase," she explained. "But this year the class was bigger than usual, and Fran had some really specific ideas of what she wanted to achieve … so she chose some of us she thought would work well together and, well, here we are!"

"It's a small crew for a film like this, right?" I asked. I knew for a fact that the other group had twice as many people in it.

Kat shrugged. "That's why we have you on board,

I guess. And Jenn," she added after a second.

Jenn, standing behind her, scowled at being forgotten.

After my interview with Kat I shadowed Derek as he put together the costumes for that afternoon, explaining for the benefit of my viewers how he chose the pieces. I also spent some time filming Tyler, who talked about the right way to light the scenes we were shooting. It was the most useful stuff I'd got all week, so I was feeling pretty pleased with myself by the time Jenn appeared with sandwiches and drinks for everyone.

Everyone except me, that is.

"Um, I think you might have forgotten something," I said as the rest of the cast and crew wandered off to eat.

Jenn looked around in an ostentatious way. "Nope. Everyone who is *working* on the film has their lunch."

I rolled my eyes at her pettiness. "Fine. I'll go grab my own."

As I stalked off towards the door, I heard Jenn mutter, "Oh, but how will we ever cope without you?" in the most sarcastic tone ever.

Matty caught up to me as I headed out.

"You OK?" he asked, around his mouthful of turkey Swiss sub.

"Your girlfriend is a right—"

"I'm not here to talk about Jenn," he interrupted. "I'm asking about you."

I shrugged. "I'm hungry. But that's easily fixed."

"It's not the only thing that needs fixing," he said, looking at me meaningfully.

I stopped walking. "Is this a 'let's make Willa and Jenn best friends' intervention? Because if so, you can head back right now."

"It's not," Matty told me. "It's a 'help Willa help herself' intervention."

"Willa is fine, thanks," I told him.

"Willa is making enemies and alienating people," Matty countered.

"Willa is getting on with her job. And she's also sick of talking about herself in the third person."

"Willa is—"

"What?" I spun round to face him in the middle of the pavement. "I'm here, every day, even though it's the holidays. I've been interviewing the cast, getting great footage *and* moving tables and holding lights. So I left Jenn to do one sandwich run. Was that so bad?"

"It's not just one sandwich run, Willa." Matty leaned against the wall that surrounded the school buildings. "You keep disappearing when we need you, arriving late or cutting out early. Remember what I said? It's not just your reputation on the line here. I vouched for you, so it's my reputation too. And you're not living up to the promises I made for you."

"Well, if someone gave me the chance to do something other than shifting furniture or holding lights, maybe I would!"

Matty carried on as if I hadn't spoken. "Even when you're here, you're focusing on your own stuff, not the film we're trying to make."

"You knew that was why I wanted to get on board with the project. You said Fran was OK with that." I wasn't going to address the other stuff about my schedule – Matty didn't need to know.

"And she is. She's looking forward to seeing the film you make."

"So what's the problem?"

Matty sighed. "You're also our production assistant. Which means, you know, doing the PA's job."

"Production assistant seems to mean dogsbody," I grumbled, annoyed to admit that Jenn had been right. "I didn't join this project to run errands. I joined it to *learn*."

"Everyone has to start somewhere, Willa."

"And I've already started! I have my own YouTube

channel, I've directed my own short pieces, like the flash mob, loads of stuff!"

"But that was just you, right? This … this is your first time working as part of a bigger team."

"So? Why does that make any difference?"

Matty squinted in the LA sunlight, not looking directly at me. "The thing is … this project really *matters* to the rest of us, Willa. We're giving it everything we've got. And, well, it doesn't seem like you are. You're not a part of the team yet."

With that, Matty turned and walked away. Leaving me staring after him, trying to process what he'd said.

Of course I was giving it everything. That was why I'd rearranged my entire spring break and got Alice to stand in for me, right? To make this happen.

Matty didn't know what he was talking about.

But that didn't stop the uneasy feeling in my stomach.

Telling myself I was just hungry, I headed off to find a sandwich. I didn't want to miss any of the action on set, after all.

Later that afternoon, I skipped out on clear-up and caught the bus down to Santa Monica to swap places with Alice again. I found her in the education suite with Jake, their heads bent together so close that his blond hair almost blurred into her darker ponytail.

I frowned. She'd had her hair down that morning when I left, so she'd obviously put it up herself. Without looking in a mirror, apparently, since it was completely lopsided. I mean, I know she wasn't *actually* me, but would it kill her to at least try to look the part?

When neither of them looked up, I cleared my throat loudly. Alice's head bobbed up first, eyes wide and startled. She smiled when she spotted me, then reached up to yank the spiral bobble from her hair.

"Is it that time already?" she asked, glancing at her bare wrist. She still hadn't got used to not having her watch, and I hadn't got used to wearing it — it was currently shoved in the front pocket of Alice's rucksack.

"Yep. You ready to go?" I asked.

Alice looked to Jake for approval. He nodded.

"I think we've done all we can here today." He smiled warmly at her. "You've done a great job. I don't think we've ever been so prepared for a vacation camp visit on the day before. Thanks, Willa."

Alice's gaze shot to meet mine as he said my name.

"That's Willa," I said, my mouth dry. "Always prepared."

Her smile rigid, Alice nodded stiffly. "I'll see you tomorrow, Jake."

Neither of us spoke as we switched clothes again in the bathroom. In fact, we didn't say anything until we were both in the car with Mum, heading home again.

"So, what's the deal with you and Jake?" I saw Mum's gaze flick to the mirror as I asked; she always likes a bit of gossip. "I just found them cosying up together in the education suite," I explained.

Alice's cheeks flamed bright red. "That's not... We were just looking through the packs for the kids visiting tomorrow! Jake asked me to do one of the introductory talks, so I wanted to make sure I had all the information right."

"That's how it starts," I teased. "It's all bonding over recycling leaflets, then suddenly you're kissing in a kayak." I twisted in my seat so I could face her properly. "I could do your make-up for you tomorrow. And your hair, if you wanted..."

"Willa!" Alice had her hands over her face now, but I could see that even her ears were pink. "Stop it. Really. Jake's a nice guy, but that's not... I don't look at him that way."

I leaned back against the car's leather seats, not wanting to push her any more if she was uncomfortable, even though I'd only been trying to help. But I couldn't help adding, "Then you must be one of the very few fifteen-year-olds in LA who doesn't want to kiss him or be him."

Alice lowered her hands. "You know me. I like to be different."

"That's true." It was one of the things I liked about her.

We drove in silence for a few minutes, while I tried to think of something else to distract me from everything Matty had said at lunchtime.

"I know!" I said, bouncing on my seat as the perfect idea came to me. "We'll have a girls' night tonight! Manicures, movies, Mexican takeaway ... and you can tell us all about Hot Jake!"

"Willa..." Alice didn't sound convinced.

"Fine," I huffed. "But can we at least still have the first three?"

Alice smiled. "Well, I do love Mexican food..."

I bounced again. "Brilliant! This is going to be great."

ALICE

Girly sleepover nights aren't really my sort of thing, but Willa seemed so excited about this one that I couldn't help but get caught up in it. Even Mrs Andrews seemed enthusiastic, swinging by a store to pick up popcorn and coming out with several new nail-varnish colours and some face-mask sheet things that I was pretty sure were going to bring my sensitive skin out in spots.

Back at the house, we all got changed into our pyjamas. Willa and I were debating which movie to watch as we came downstairs to the cinema room, but it turned out that Willa's mum had another plan.

"Jacinta sent through the photos from the shoot!" She pressed a button on the remote and the huge screen burst into life, displaying a photo of the three of us wearing funny hats. "I thought you could look through them together before the movie? Choose a few to send over to Alice's dad?"

"Perfect!" Willa hopped into a seat in the front row, pulling her feet up under her. "But first we have to get comfortable."

I took the seat next to her and, at the same moment, we pressed the buttons that made the padded leather chairs recline, bringing up a footrest at the front.

"These chairs are amazing!" I couldn't have imagined someone having an actual cinema in their house until I came to LA. Now, it seemed perfectly normal.

Mrs Andrews handed Willa the remote. "You girls start looking through the photos, I'll go call for the takeaway."

"*Told* you the photoshoot was a good idea," Willa said, as shot after shot of the two of us messing around filled the screen. We were laughing or smiling in every one of them, and the brightly coloured accessories we'd tried on each other popped against the white of the studio wall.

"You were right," I admitted. "Now, which one of these shall I send over to Dad and Mabel?"

Willa reset the slideshow to the start, and we looked through them more slowly, laughing at the faces we were pulling in some of them. Willa's favourite was the one where she'd jammed a bright pink fedora on to my head. Mine was one of us sitting together on an electric blue sofa, chatting.

We'd finally narrowed down the photos to send Dad to thirteen, when Mrs Andrews' voice echoed down the stairs. "Alice! Phone for you!"

I jumped up. "That'll be Dad. I forgot to phone tonight!"

Every day since I'd arrived I'd video-called home, just like I'd promised. The time difference made it tricky, but if I called at breakfast time they were usually just finishing work and had time to chat. Sometimes I called at lunch time, when it was evening for them. But today, I'd forgotten. It had to be two in the morning back in London!

Racing upstairs to the kitchen, I took the cordless phone from Willa's mum.

"Dad? I'm so sorry I forgot to call!"

On the other end of the phone, Dad laughed. "That's OK, Starfish! I figured you were probably busy, but your mobile was going straight to voicemail, and we have some exciting news to share…"

I pulled my phone from my pocket. "Dead battery," I confirmed. "Sorry. What's the news?"

Last time they'd had big news it was that they were getting married. I'd just about got over that shock by now.

"We've bought a house!"

A strange, cold feeling shivered through me. "What?"

"Mabel and I went to see it today and we just knew – it's our dream home. So we made an offer there and then! We just know you're going to love it."

"But … we've been looking at houses together for months. What was so different about this one?"

It wasn't the question I wanted to ask. What I *wanted* to ask was, *How can you have found OUR home without me there?*

All along, Dad and Mabel had talked about the new house being the first home we'd all share together. But now they'd gone and chosen it without even letting me see it.

"Oh, you'll see what we mean when you see it, Alice. It's just perfect for the three of us. It really is." Dad paused. "Aren't you excited?"

He wanted me to be, I knew that. And *I* wanted to be too, really. A new house meant my own bedroom again – not sharing the box room with all Mabel's old research files and her desk.

It just felt wrong, was all.

"Of course I am," I lied. "Send me over the details. Photos and stuff?"

"Mabel's emailing them right now," Dad said.

In the background I heard Mabel shouting, "The bedroom with the blue walls will be yours!"

They'd even picked out my bedroom for me. Great. "Tell Mabel I'll look out for it."

Dad chatted for a bit longer about the garden. "It's only small, but I reckon we can manage a barbecue." And the fact that the house was only a short walk from the Tube … but I wasn't really listening. All I could think was that my future was being decided without me.

"Everything OK?" Mrs Andrews asked as I hung up.

"Fine." I forced a smile. "Dad and Mabel have found a new house for us."

"Brilliant! You can tell us all about it over tacos."

WILLA

Something was up with Alice.

She'd barely touched her tacos, hadn't laughed at any of the right places in the movie we'd chosen after we finished looking through the photos, and had let me paint her nails a bright orange I knew she'd normally hate.

With the mood of our girly night definitely off, we headed up to my room as soon as the movie finished. While Alice cleaned her teeth and washed her face, I pulled up my footage from the day's filming and did some basic cleaning up and editing on it.

Eventually Alice emerged from the bathroom and threw herself on to her bed without even saying goodnight.

I paused my footage. "OK, what's going on with you tonight? Was it the call from your dad? Mum said something about a house?" It had been at the same time as the food had arrived, so I hadn't caught *all* the details.

"Mmm mm mmmmmm mmm mmmmm m

mmm mmmm," Alice mumbled into the pillow.

I jumped up and pulled the pillow out from under her. "Let's try that again?"

Alice sat up, looking severely grumpy. "Dad and Mabel have bought us a new house."

"And that's bad because…?"

"It's not."

"Except you're *clearly* in a mood about it," I pointed out. "I thought you'd be thrilled to get out of Mabel's tiny flat." It had been small enough when it was just me and Mabel last summer. I couldn't imagine how cramped it was with all three of them and their stuff there.

"I am. I mean, I will be. It's just…" Alice sighed. "I'm probably being stupid."

Alice was many things, but *never* stupid.

Settling cross-legged on the end of her bed, I put on my best listening face. "What is it? Is it in the wrong end of town? Is it haunted? Is your room decorated with Disney princesses?"

"None of the above. I haven't even seen the details yet. Mabel was going to email over some photos and stuff. But that's not really the point."

"Then what is?"

"They chose our new family home without me."

Oh.

Alice's mum had died a few years ago and she'd struggled with accepting Mabel in their lives at all. They got along well now, I thought, but still. The idea of Mabel and her dad moving on, and leaving the memory of her mum and their old life behind, must have been tough.

"My parents sold our family home when they got divorced," I said slowly, thinking my way through what it was I wanted to say. "Since then, it's mostly been rented flats in cities where they work, and I shuffle between them depending on whose turn it is to have me. Then Mum and I came here to LA and borrowed this place, which is fabulous, but it isn't really home."

"Do you wish your parents would get back together?" Alice asked.

Did I? "I guess… I wish they'd never got divorced in the first place. But they both seem happier now. Mum's career has really taken off, we get to live in Hollywood, and Dad visits a lot … so I don't know. It's complicated."

"Yeah," Alice said heavily. "It's just weird to think that they chose *our* home without me. You know?"

"I do. But think about it – in three years or so you'll

be off to university and they'll still be living in it."

"I just can't imagine a home I haven't seen before. It feels a bit like being sent to stay with Mabel last year when I'd never even met her."

I smiled. "And we all know how that ended up."

Alice laughed, which was exactly what I'd been angling for.

"Maybe it'll feel more real once you've seen the photos," I suggested. "Ooh, we can get on Pinterest and start designing your new room!"

"Yeah, OK," Alice agreed. "Tomorrow."

"Tomorrow," I promised.

ALICE

The next morning I was too busy fretting about the vacation camp visit to think much more about the new house. I knew Willa was right when she pointed out that I should be glad to be getting out of Mabel's tiny box room. In fact, I should be grateful to have a home at all. Not to mention the fact that it meant we wouldn't have to spend *every* weekend viewing houses any more. Besides, standing up in front of thirty children and telling them about keeping our oceans clean and reducing plastic use was a far more immediate terror.

What if the kids didn't listen? What if nobody cared what I had to say? What if I got everything wrong and made a complete fool of myself?

When I told Willa my fears over breakfast, she rolled her eyes. But later, just as she was about to leave the Shore Thing, she put both hands on my shoulders and looked in my eyes.

"Remember, when you're up there, you're not Alice Wright. You're Willa Andrews. And she's not scared of some kids in a classroom, OK?"

I couldn't help but smile. "OK."

It wasn't until I was standing up there in front of the group, Jake smiling encouragingly from the back, that I realized she'd chosen her favourite outfit for me today – a short denim dungaree dress with a bright pink T-shirt and matching Converse high tops. She'd told me before it was her 'I'll show them' outfit.

I took a deep breath, smiled at the kids, and began to speak.

"Our oceans cover seventy-one per cent of the Earth's surface, and they hold ninety-seven per cent of the planet's water – I think we can all agree that makes them pretty important, right?" A few nods – I guessed they'd probably already learned that in school. "Especially since *we* – you and I – are made of about sixty per cent water too." A couple of kids looked surprised at that, but more nodded.

"OK, but here's another important water fact for you," I went on. "Ninety-nine per cent of the living space on Earth is in the oceans."

That one got a few gasps at least. Then one kid shouted out, "And it's wasted on a few fish!" His friends laughed, of course.

I could see Jake giving me a concerned look from

the corner of the room, and I knew he was worrying that he'd given me too much responsibility too fast.

But now I was up here... Today, I was Willa Andrews, all the way down to my pink Converse. But more than that, I was Alice Wright. Daughter of Jon Wright, marine biologist. I'd grown up with starfish in a tank in my bedroom. I knew what I was talking about, and that gave me even more confidence than Willa's clothes.

I could do this.

"All right," I said to the joker of the group. "How many species of animals do you think live in our oceans?"

He shrugged. "A couple of hundred."

"Anyone else?" I asked.

"It's a lot more than that," one girl said, shaking her head. "Like, hundreds of thousands."

"A million?" someone else shouted out.

Right then, I was so grateful for my dad's marine biology lectures at the dining table. For every talk of his I ever sat in on. Because I had the answer right at the tip of my tongue.

"There are 228,450 known species in our oceans — and there could be as many as two million more that we don't even know about yet! And personally, I'd like to keep looking after our oceans so we can find out about all two million of them. How about you?"

"Yeah!" one kid shouted, and others joined in with nods and yells.

I clapped my hands together. "Great! Then let's get started."

"That was brilliant." Jake wrapped an arm around my shoulders as the camp leaders and Shore Thing volunteers herded the kids towards the deck to eat their packed lunches before the beach walk that afternoon. "*You* were brilliant."

"I don't know about brilliant. But at least I didn't fall over the desk or claim that climate change was just a theory."

Jake laughed. "The kids were really engaged. I heard a few of them sounding genuinely excited to explore the beach habitats this afternoon. I think you deserve a reward," he added suddenly. "How do you fancy taking a trip?"

"Ice cream on the pier again?" I guessed. It *would* be nice to get out and have some fun. Now the immediate terror of my talk had passed, my worries about the new house were creeping back in again. And Jake,

I had to admit, was an *excellent* distraction.

When Jake smiled, his dimples showed. And his eyes seemed to, well, dance. It was a phrase I'd read before but never really understood until now. "I was thinking we could even try the Pacific Wheel for something a bit more exciting," he said.

"We don't need to help with the beach walk?"

"I think we've earned a break. You've definitely put in more than your mandatory four hours a day this week!"

I hoped my smile hid the surprise I felt. I'd totally forgotten, for a moment, that I was supposed to be there as a punishment. I was having far too much fun helping out at the Shore Thing to think about that.

Santa Monica Pier wasn't *exactly* like the piers back home in Britain. For starters, Southend-on-Sea definitely didn't have people selling hot dogs on sticks, and I'd never even tried funnel cake before Jake persuaded me to.

Part of the pier was taken over by an amusement park, with rides and sideshow games that were more familiar. I had fun tossing rings and shooting water cannons – I even won Jake a giant octopus stuffed toy that he carried around with him for the rest of the day. Eventually we stopped beside the giant Ferris wheel and a rollercoaster.

"Do you really want me to ride on that?" I asked, squinting up at the huge wheel silhouetted against the blue of the Californian sky.

"Not a fan of heights?" he guessed.

"Not really," I admitted.

"Me neither." He gave a relaxed shrug then reached out to take my hand. "Come on. I think I know something you might like better."

Jake led me into a sandy-coloured building with arched blue windows and doors. I caught sight of the words above the door as we entered. "Merry-go-round?"

"Look," Jake said, and I gasped.

Inside was the most fantastic old-fashioned carousel – the sort with painted horses with names drawn on their saddles that go up and down to old-time music. As it turned, the kids and adults riding it whooped and called out, laughing over the music as they spun around.

"More your speed?" Jake asked with a smile. The carousel had just come to a stop, and people were slipping down from their horses to be replaced by the next riders. "You want to take a ride?"

I hadn't really expected Jake to climb on too. But as I settled on to my silver galloper with a shining lilac mane, he jumped up on to the black horse beside me.

"You like the carousel?" I asked.

Jake shrugged. "I like spending time with you."

I looked away, my heart suddenly pounding. I'd told Willa I didn't think of Jake like that. Yet it seemed I wasn't completely immune to the fact that this gorgeous guy seemed to want to hang out with me. I'd thought, because he didn't give me those immediate, overwhelming crush-like feelings I'd had with Antonio last summer, that I didn't see him that way at all. That we'd just be friends with things in common, like I was with Hal back in London. But the more I got to know Jake, the more time I spent with him, the more I liked him. And as much as I tried to ignore Willa's teasing ... I had to admit, he really *was* gorgeous.

Did that mean this was something more than a crush? I wasn't sure.

But I knew one thing for certain: Jake thought I was someone I wasn't.

ALICE

How long did it take you to forgive me, really, when you found out the truth last summer?

LUCA

Um ... why?

ALICE

Just curious.

LUCA

You're pretending to be Willa again, aren't you? I knew it!

ALICE

Why on earth would I do that?

LUCA

Because Willa convinced you it would be a good idea somehow.

ALICE

Actually, it was the other way around.

ALICE

So. How long?

LUCA

I think ... until I understood. And even then, I didn't exactly agree with what you'd done. But I understood why you thought you needed to do it. So even though I was angry, I could start forgiving you.

LUCA

So, why are you doing it this time?

ALICE

Honestly? I'm not sure even I know any more.

ALICE

Except ... I really don't want to stop.

WILLA

Friday – our last day of filming at the school – wasn't any better than the last few days. Principal Carter visited again, so I spent twenty minutes hiding in the janitor's closet and hoping no one noticed I was missing. Of course, they did.

"I don't even know why you bother showing up at all," Jenn spat at me, when I finally emerged.

"Yeah, well we all know *exactly* why you're here," I shot back, with a meaningful look at where Matty and Fran had their heads bent together over the script.

Jenn's face paled and she stalked off without responding. Part of me felt bad for bringing it up, but mostly I was just annoyed that nothing seemed to be going the way I'd planned.

That afternoon Fran changed her mind three times about how she wanted to block one of the scenes, which meant changing the lighting and cameras too – and for me and Jenn, shifting more furniture and holding more lights. I rolled my eyes at Matty as I played lampstand yet again, but he just shook his head at me. Apparently the fact that my arm was completely numb by this point was of no concern to anyone except me.

At least me and Alice would have the weekend off from filming and the Shore Thing Project. I daydreamed about all the cool LA stuff I could show her, as I held Tyler's light in position long enough for him to fix it. When Fran called a wrap for the week, I shot out of there quicker than anyone, fishing out my phone to text Alice as I waited for the bus.

Before I could send my text though, one pinged up. From Mum.

Finished early today so heading over to the Shore Thing as soon as I'm changed to pick you both up.

My eyes widened as I read it again.

Every second of the bus ride back to Santa Monica was excruciating. I bounced anxiously in my seat, cursing LA traffic the whole way. Then, as the bus pulled in to my stop, I shot through the doors and ran to the Shore Thing offices in record time – only to find that Alice wasn't there.

"Oh, I think Jake and Willa went off to explore a bit together," Darla told me, when I'd fought my way through a crowd of young kids with rubbish bags to find her office. "I'm surprised they didn't call you, Alice."

I ducked my head so my hair was in my face as she looked up from her computer screen. "No worries. I'll go wait out on the deck."

I scurried off again before she got a really good look at me, channelling my inner nervous Alice. I had to find her. And quick.

Where *was* she? Well, with Hot Jake, obviously. So much for her not thinking of him that way if she'd run off to spend the afternoon with him without even *texting* me to say she'd be late…

I checked Alice's watch. Mum would be on her way by now. I needed to make a decision.

I pulled out my phone and tapped out a quick message.

Thanks, but I'm going to take Alice to see the pier this afternoon, so we'll get the bus home later. OK?

And then I waited, drumming my fingers along the rail of the deck, to see who I'd hear from first, Mum or Alice.

After what seemed like forever, my phone vibrated so hard it jumped on the wooden rail, but I grabbed it before it could fall into the sand below.

OK. See you at home. Text me when you're on the bus. Mum xxx

I let out a breath as my heart rate returned to normal. First problem dealt with. Second problem…

Pulling up the stalker app we'd set up on our phones after the last time Alice disappeared with Jake (OK, the Find My Friends app), I searched for Alice's dot. I should have done this sooner, but in the heat of the moment I'd forgotten all about it.

She was on the pier. Of course.

I kept an eye on her dot as I walked towards the pier, noting the moment it started heading in my direction. So she hadn't forgotten about me completely, then. Great.

I spotted them before they saw me. I stood on the sand with my arms folded and waited.

Their heads were bent together as they walked, and I could see Alice's wide smile even at a distance. And Jake… Well, he couldn't look away from her for a moment. Whatever Alice had said about it not being like that between them, my eyes told me different.

Alice looked up and saw me, her smile falling away. Turning quickly to Jake she muttered something, then began running towards me, Jake keeping pace beside her.

"Is everything OK? I'm so sorry we're late. We kind of … lost track of time." She glanced up at Jake as she said that. I couldn't quite see Alice being too busy kissing a hot guy to remember her friends existed, but then she wasn't being *Alice* right now. She was being me.

And honestly? I couldn't totally promise that I wouldn't do that. Which didn't make me feel any better about the whole situation.

"Your mum messaged to say she'd pick us up today, but since I couldn't find you I texted her and told her we'd get the bus home," I said shortly, forgetting for a second that obviously 'Willa' should have been the one to text her mum. Jake frowned a little in confusion, but didn't say anything.

"Right. OK. Um, do you want to head off now?" Alice looked a little taken aback by my cold tone.

Good. I wanted her to know how cross I was. How close we'd come to getting caught. If I hadn't got here early, hadn't been able to text Mum before she left to pick us up…

Neither Alice nor I made any move to go anywhere, and eventually Jake got the hint.

"I guess I'll see you tomorrow then, Willa." He gave Alice a secret smile before he headed up the beach towards the Shore Thing building. A smile she returned with one just as soft as she watched him walk away.

Oh, this was not good at all. The last thing I needed was Alice blowing *everything* for us both, just because she had a crush on Jake.

I needed to put a stop to this.

Right now.

ALICE

Willa waited until Jake was well out of earshot before she turned on me. "Where were you? Why didn't you text me? I thought Mum was going to show up and blow the whole thing! What were you *thinking*?"

"Willa, I'm sorry. I told you, we just lost track of time a bit."

"Because you were with *Jake.*" She shook her head at me like a disapproving teacher. "I know we joked about him being Hot Jake, Alice, but that was just for fun! You can't really be getting into anything with him, can you? You *know* it's going to end badly when he finds out that you're not really me."

I stared at her as her words sank in. "Because of course no guy would actually want to spend time with *me*, Alice, would they?"

"That's not what I meant!" Willa yelled. "I just don't want you getting in too deep with Jake. Or blowing the whole plan because of him."

"That's what this is *really* about, isn't it?" I shot back. "You don't care about me or Jake. You just don't want to get caught and have to stop work on your film!"

"I don't want either of us to get caught!" Willa said. "You can't tell me your dad wouldn't lose it if he found out you'd been pretending to be me again."

"But we *didn't* get caught," I said. "We weren't even *that* late. I think I'd have made it back before your mum got here, anyway."

"And what if you hadn't? What if she'd got here and you weren't here? What then?" She paced across the sand, her hands on her hips.

I'd seen Willa grumpy, happy, sulky, excited, over-confident and even a little unsure before. But I'd never seen her angry. Not like this.

I frowned. "Well, then you'd have been able to tell her that you'd been volunteering like you were supposed to and that I'd gone for a wander with Jake and wasn't back yet."

"And when you finally showed up *wearing my clothes?*" There was genuine fury in her voice now.

"I don't know, Willa! You could have told her you lent me your favourite dress so I'd be more confident hanging out with Jake, or something. You're the improv expert."

"That's not the point," she snapped, and I knew she was irritated she hadn't thought of it first. "You were supposed to be *here*. Now I've had to lie to Mum and we have to get the bus home and—"

"Wait." That was enough for me. Yes, I should have been back when I promised. But if Willa was going to try to make me feel guilty for *her* lying to her mum, that was when she crossed the line. "I think you've forgotten who is covering for who here. I'm the one who's pretending to be someone else every day – again!"

"It was YOUR idea!" Willa shouted. "And you can't tell me you're not *loving* pretending to be me."

I ignored her and carried on. "Who here is having to lie to nice people about everything? I'm the one who is doing *your* punishment for you, all so you can go work on a film project you've done nothing but moan about since you started. So, I'm sorry if you were worried about me blowing your cover, but honestly? I *deserved* an afternoon off having fun. In case you've forgotten, I'm *supposed* to be on holiday."

And with that I stormed past her, heading in the direction of the bus stop.

After a few moments, she followed. I didn't look at her. She didn't look at me.

We waited for the bus in silence. It rumbled to a stop in front of us a few minutes later, and we boarded in silence. And then we sat side by side in silence as it drove through the Santa Monica streets, back towards Willa's house.

I didn't exactly expect her to say sorry; apologies weren't really Willa's style, especially when she still probably didn't think she was in the wrong. But I wasn't going to say sorry either. Not when all I'd done was try to make the best of the situation *she'd* put me in.

I'd had a lovely afternoon with Jake, and I wasn't going to apologize for that.

We were halfway to our stop when she turned to me, suddenly jerking her head up. "We haven't swapped clothes."

"What do you want to do?" I asked.

"We'll get off here. Come on."

Grabbing my hand, Willa yanked me with her as we headed for the bus doors, ready to jump off at the next stop. The doors swished opened and we both hopped down. Willa dropped my hand and headed towards a brightly coloured café, without looking back to see if I was following.

The café was some sort of milkshake and waffle place. Willa bypassed the queue and made straight for the bathrooms. We swapped our clothes back with as little conversation and contact as possible. Then, when I thought we'd head back out to catch the next bus, Willa joined the queue. "What flavour milkshake do you want?"

I hid my smile. In Willa terms, that was basically a grovelling apology.

"Vanilla, please."

I grabbed the table by the window and Willa joined me a few minutes later with two tall milkshake glasses: my vanilla, and chocolate with whipped cream and marshmallows for her.

"Thanks."

As I put the straw in my mouth and sucked up the dairy goodness, I met Willa's gaze across the table and knew the next move was mine.

"I'm sorry I was late back this afternoon. I should have texted you."

"I'm sorry I lost it with you. I know you're only doing this to help me out. I just… I really didn't mean what you thought I meant, about you and Jake. I was just worried about you getting your heart broken. Or breaking his when you disappear next week."

"We're friends. We just hung out at the pier this afternoon, that's all. He took me on the carousel.

He said … he said he likes spending time with me."

Willa's eyes widened. "That's what a guy says when he really *likes* you."

"As a friend."

"Not *just* as a friend."

"It was nice to hang out with him," I said, not really wanting to talk about it any more. At least, not until I'd figured out how I felt about it all. "But I came to LA to hang out with *you*. And this feels like the first time we've managed to do that at all."

Willa looked a little guilty at my words, then she brightened. "Well, that changes tomorrow! It's Saturday. We can do anything you want. Go anywhere, see anything. So, what do you want to do?"

I thought about my Los Angeles guidebook, sitting on my bedside table in Willa's room, Post-it flags bursting out of almost every page.

I grinned. "Everything."

WILLA

Normally I like to sleep in on the weekends. But this wasn't a normal weekend.

This was Willa and Alice's Crazy Day of LA Fun.

Mum looked a little surprised to see us both dressed and ready for breakfast before nine o'clock, but Alice waved her guidebook at her and she got it quick enough.

"Where are you going to start?" Mum asked as I toasted us bagels.

I shot her a look of disbelief. "There's only one place *to* start."

"Ah, of course," Mum said. "Hollywood Boulevard," we all chorused together.

"Well, you two have fun and, Willa, regular check-ins, please." Mum grabbed her bag and, as an apparent afterthought, stole half my bagel. "I'll be on set this morning but I'm free this afternoon if you want me to meet you or pick you up."

"Thanks, Mum." I looked across at Alice. "But I think we'll be OK."

Milkshakes the day before had gone a long way to

repairing things between us after our first big fight. I hoped today would do the rest.

Incredibly, this was the first time it had ever just been the two of us together.

Today was *our* day.

Mum pressed a kiss on the top of my head. "Use the credit card for food and if you want to take a tour or anything, but try to keep the impulse buys to a minimum, yeah?"

"OK." 'Minimum' wasn't a *total* ban on shopping. That was something.

Getting anywhere in LA takes too long. We hopped on the bus heading the opposite way to normal, changed once, and almost an hour later – an hour of Alice reading me things I already knew from her guidebook – arrived at Hollywood Boulevard.

When you think about LA, after you picture the famous Hollywood sign itself, the boulevard is probably what you see. It's the place where the names of celebrities are immortalized forever in the brass stars of the Walk of Fame.

"So, who do you want to see first?" I asked Alice as we stood outside the TCL Chinese Theatre, with the crowds waiting to put their hands and feet in the prints left in the forecourt by old-time celebrities.

Alice turned from where she'd been studying the iconic building. Her face was bright with excitement. For a moment, I felt a pang that the whole of our week hadn't been like this. If I hadn't had the film or the punishment, we could have been doing this from day one.

But we were doing it now, and I wasn't going to waste a minute of it moping about things we *hadn't* done.

Alice whipped a Post-it Note from her guidebook. "I made a list."

"You are the most organized tourist ever."

"I don't want to miss anything! Right, stars I want to see… Buzz Aldrin and Neil Armstrong."

"Aren't they, well, astronauts? Not celebrities?"

"They were the first people on the moon," Alice pointed out. "I think they get to be both. And they have stars at Hollywood and Vine."

"That's the other end of the boulevard. We can walk up there last," I told her. "Who else?"

"Um, Carole King – she was my mum's favourite singer. Oh, and Ella Fitzgerald, for my dad. And…" She blushed slightly. "Daniel Radcliffe. Obviously."

"Harry Potter? OK." I pulled up the app on my phone to tell me where each of the stars were. There are over two and a half thousand, so you can't exactly just keep an eye out and hope.

Along the way, we entertained ourselves by spotting names we recognized – and looking up a few we'd never heard of. It was fun, chatting and laughing, being drawn along by the crowds, our arms linked together so we couldn't get separated.

With Alice there, it was like I was seeing my new city for the first time, all over again.

We reached Vine Street and the stars of Alice's astronauts, snapped a couple of photos, then turned around and headed back again. On the way we debated which houses we – and our friends and family – would be sorted into at Hogwarts.

"Hal would definitely be a Ravenclaw," I declared. "What about Luca?"

"Gryffindor," Alice said decisively. "Brave and loyal. Like Achilles and Hercules."

"The heroes from those old movies?" I asked, confused by the connection.

"The donkeys on your aunt's farm," she explained. "Didn't I tell you about the donkeys?"

She launched into another story about her time in Italy as I guided her towards the Hollywood and Highland shopping centre – and the best churros I'd ever tasted.

"I still can't quite believe we actually swapped places last summer," Alice said, licking sugar from her fingers. "I mean, I also can't believe we're doing it again..."

I laughed. "Is it so bad, being me?"

"No." Alice's smile slipped a bit, and I wondered what she was thinking about. But it didn't look like much of a happy thought, so I didn't push.

Jumping to my feet, I wiped my hands on my jeans and picked up Alice's guidebook. "So, what do you want to do next? Get a tattoo on Sunset Strip like all the celebs? Visit some museums and art galleries?" I flicked through the pages until one Post-it Note jumped out at me. "Ooh! No, we're definitely doing this." I grabbed her hand and pulled her up. "Follow me!"

ALICE

"A bus tour?" I had to say, it didn't really sound like the sort of thing that would get Willa excited. I'd been on an open-top bus tour around Cambridge and mostly it was just looking at old buildings while the guide told you interesting facts about them. *I'd* found it interesting, but I wasn't completely sure Willa would.

"A bus tour of famous people's houses," she corrected as we queued for tickets.

"Mabel told me about these tours," I said, flicking through the leaflet Willa had handed me. "She said she did one when she was out here and it was fun." Mabel had a kind of fascination with other people's houses, though. I think it came from living in tiny London flats for so long.

She'd been so excited, looking around houses with me and Dad, trying to find the right one for our new family of three. I couldn't help but wonder how it would have felt to walk into the *right* one at last, and know it was going to be our home.

We collected our headsets and boarded the bus,

settling into seats about halfway down. Willa let me take the window seat for the best view.

The bus took us away from Hollywood Boulevard and towards the homes of the rich and famous, up in Beverly Hills. Our tour guide, Benny, told hilarious anecdotes about celebrity sightings gone wrong, and the time his passengers got to see Al Pacino putting out the rubbish in his dressing gown, keeping us all giggling as we crept along through the LA traffic.

Willa and I whispered to each other with every house we passed, as everyone on the bus pressed themselves against the windows to try to get a glimpse of a celeb. (We didn't see any, even though the women in front of us were absolutely certain they saw Keanu Reeves.)

"Whose house is that?" I asked, not recognizing the name Benny said.

Willa shrugged. "Some old-guy star who just does cameos these days, I reckon. Ooh, but we might get to see Katy Perry's place!"

"That one doesn't even look as big as the place you're staying," I whispered at one of the stops.

"Yeah, but that's not actually our house," Willa pointed out. "We're just borrowing it until it's time to move back to Britain again."

I hadn't really thought about Willa and me living in the same country.

"Maybe your mum will move to London," I said, suddenly excited at the idea. "You could go to the same school as me!"

"That would be pretty awesome," Willa agreed.

"Would you like to have a home of your own with your mum?" I asked, still thinking about *my* prospective new home.

Willa waggled her head from side to side as she thought. "I guess so," she said. "I mean, I like moving around different places, but it might be nice to stay somewhere for a while. And we can't decorate at Harrison's place – I'd like to decorate my own room again. But any place Mum picks is going to feel weird without Dad in it too."

"I get that." The tug of sadness I always felt when I thought of my mum wasn't as bad these days. There was more of a reminder of how happy we'd all been together as a family, as well as the sadness at her loss. "The first place Dad and I lived without Mum was so strange."

"And now you get a new home with your dad and Mabel." Willa gave me a sideways look. "You feeling any better about that yet?"

I shrugged. "I don't know. I guess I just don't feel part of it, out here. Maybe it'll be better when I get home."

"Probably." She looked out of the window at another massive mansion. "Anyway, it seems to me that the only thing that makes all these places famous is who lives in them. And the only thing that makes a place home is the people you live there with. Right?"

"Yeah," I replied. "Right." Maybe London would feel more like home if Willa moved there too. I'd like that.

As the bus pulled away from the last of the celebrity homes, it started heading up into the hills behind LA.

"Do you think we'd hang out and be friends if we were in school together?" I asked. Willa and I had very different day-to-day school experiences. She probably didn't spend every lunch break in the library, for instance. And I was never going to be up on stage as part of the Drama Club.

"Now? Absolutely." Willa spoke with the kind of certainty I could rarely manage about anything. "I mean, if we'd met at school ... maybe not so much. But now ... you're basically my best friend, Alice. Even if you do live thousands of miles away. *Of course* we'd hang out."

I looked down at the guidebook in my hands, a little embarrassed. "You're basically my best friend too. You and Luca. Not sure what it says about me that I can't find a friend who actually lives in the same country as me…"

"That you have excellent taste and hold out for the best," Willa said, putting on a snooty voice that made us both laugh.

"I'm glad we got to hang out today," I told her.

"Me too. And I *am* sorry we haven't had so much time together. I can't believe that this time next week you'll be packing to go home."

"Maybe we can find some ways to hang out more this week?" I suggested.

Willa nodded vigorously. "For definite. Actually, Fran has us filming down at the beach nearer to Santa Monica this week anyway, so it should be loads easier for me to sneak between the two."

"Brilliant!"

With a sly smile, Willa added, "As long as you've got time, in between hanging out with Jake, of course."

I rolled my eyes. "I told you. Jake's great, but it's you I came to LA to see. OK?"

That made her smile. "OK. Good."

"Besides … I can't really relax around Jake. Not the

way I can with you. When I'm with you, I'm just me again. With Jake … I'm some sort of a Willa-Alice hybrid. Like, I'm still a bit me, because I'm interested in everything the Shore Thing is doing, and I haven't completely forgotten all the marine biology and ocean conservation stuff I've learned from Dad. But I'm wearing your clothes and standing up in front of people giving presentations – which I'd never be able to do if I was just Alice."

Willa frowned. "But … that *was* you up there talking. I mean, Jake might still be calling you by the wrong name, but it wasn't exactly my clothes that made you able to give that presentation to a room full of strange kids. That was all you."

I shrugged. "I mean, the information was all me. But the confidence … that felt more like Willa."

"Like you were acting," Willa said slowly. "Playing the part of me."

"Just like we planned."

This was what I'd wanted, right? To come to LA and find that confidence I only seemed to have when I was pretending to be Willa.

Except everything about LA felt like a film, a production. Like the set behind me might disappear at any moment and I'd go back to being just Alice again. I couldn't quite imagine still being the person Jake knew, back in London again.

Would he still be interested in me if he knew who I really was? I couldn't be sure. And that, more than anything, made me want to hold back from examining my feelings for him too carefully.

The bus turned another corner, and suddenly we saw it close up – or as close as we were able to get. The famous Hollywood sign, shining bright in the sunlight above the city.

A city people had been coming to for decades to chase their dreams. To make their fantasies real. To be the people they always believed they could be.

Just like I had.

And maybe I was getting there, just not quite the way I expected. Because the longer I pretended to be Willa, the more I started to feel like me again.

WILLA

Alice was quiet the rest of the way, after the bus wended its way back along Sunset Strip to Hollywood Boulevard again, and we climbed wearily aboard another bus to start the journey home. I figured she was just tired – we both were. But the kind of tired you feel after a really fun day, so that was OK.

The next day was Easter Sunday, so we had chocolate pancakes for breakfast and Easter eggs for lunch. Mum tried to cook a proper Sunday roast for us all, but since it went about as well as her usual attempts, we were glad of the extra chocolate.

After a fun and relaxed weekend, I headed back to join the others on set down at Santa Monica on Monday morning with a lot more hope than I'd left with on Friday. We were filming up in Palisades Park, and fortunately it was some of the modern-day scenes, which was way easier.

The sunshine meant the lighting wasn't too bad either, and everyone seemed to be in a good mood after the weekend. I even managed to smile at Jenn when she arrived. She didn't smile back, of course, but at least I'd *tried*. Maybe I was still feeling a bit guilty about my comment on Friday.

Matty's words had also stayed with me over our days off, and I'd thought about them even more as I'd talked with Alice about how she and Jake were working together over at the Shore Thing Project. As much as I really wanted to focus on my behind-the-scenes documentary, I wanted to be part of the team too. Like Alice had become at the Shore Thing.

Matty was right. I'd promised to pull my weight on the film, and I would.

So I threw myself into Being Helpful – although I still made sure to keep my mini camera handy to shoot any moments I just couldn't miss. I even went and did the coffee run that morning so that Jenn didn't have to, which also meant I actually got the iced latte I wanted instead of a) nothing or b) a bitter, black Americano, which was all Jenn would ever bring me.

On my return, I found the whole cast and crew gathered around the props trolley, all talking over each other.

"What's happened?" I asked as I started handing out the drinks.

Everybody looked at Jenn. Except for Matty, who

had one arm around her shoulder in a comforting way and was staring straight at the trolley. I followed his gaze and saw the problem immediately.

With *Now and Then* being set in two time periods, Fran had come up with a few visual techniques for linking the stories together. Things like having photos of Bethany and Polly in their 1980s outfits on the wall in one of the modern scenes. There were also some props that crossed over between both stories – the most important of which was a book.

This book – a paperback original of *Home from Eden*, Beatrix Frost's first novel that Fran had filched from her grandma's bookcase – was the book Polly was reading when she met Bethany for the first time. It was what helped them bond. And the idea was that now, in the 2020 scenes, Kat had found the book on *her* gran's bookshelf and was reading it to Finn while they hung out at the Palisades. The book featured in at least half the scenes we still had to shoot, including the all-important final scene on the beach.

Except the book was wrecked.

"What happened to it?" I asked in a whisper as Fran took her coffee from me.

"Jenn thought it needed to look older." Fran's words were clipped, like she was barely holding her anger in.

"Because it wouldn't be realistic if it looked exactly the same in 2020 as it had in 1988," Matty added defensively. "Which makes total sense."

Fran whirled round to face him and Jenn. "Yes, Matty, please explain to me again how tipping coffee on the most important prop in the whole film was a *good* idea. I'm not sure I quite understood the first time round."

I winced at the fury in her voice. Looking down at the book I could see where the coffee had curled the pages and stained the cover.

"She didn't tip coffee on it!" Matty argued back. "She asked me if I thought it needed ageing and I agreed – as director of photography. So she artfully used coffee grounds and a paintbrush to add some colour to the edge of the pages and—"

"And then knocked the whole cup of coffee over the book!" Fran finished with a yell.

"Not on purpose!" Matty shouted back.

Jenn had her hands over her face, her shoulders shaking as she cried silent tears. Sympathy welled up in me. I might have been a bit of an outcast on the film, but it hadn't escaped my notice that Jenn was too – even though she was working much harder than me at trying to fit in. And now she'd screwed up, it didn't look like anyone else was inclined to forgive her, even if it *had* been an accident.

Which meant it was up to me to help her.

"I can fix this," I said. "All we need is another book, right? So, you guys get on with filming the scenes that don't need the book, and I'll go fetch another one."

"It has to be exactly the same edition." Fran's voice held a note of warning, but I detected at least a little hope behind it too. "If it doesn't look the same, the whole thing is ruined."

"Like the book," Tyler muttered.

"It's a novel by a famous British author. I'm sure I can find one. You can get anything on the internet these days. Just leave it to me." Nobody looked at all certain about entrusting me with this task. "Guys, I can do it!" I insisted.

Fran looked around the cast and crew, then shrugged. "Well, what have we got to lose? Right. Willa, you find a replacement prop. Everyone else, we'll shift to filming the next Palisades scene instead, so let's get costumes and location all set." She clapped her hands together. "Let's move!"

Guessing that meant me too, I grabbed my bag and my iced coffee, and headed for somewhere with a decent internet signal. Time to do what I was best at: shopping.

Except this was *book* shopping – something I wasn't exactly renowned for. But luckily, I knew a girl who was...

WILLA

OK, so if you needed to find an old book really quickly, what would you do?

HAL

I'd ask Alice.

WILLA

Of course I'm asking Alice. But she's busy right now and not answering her phone, so I'm trying to make a start on my own.

HAL

Try Amazon. Did you know, once upon a time they *only* sold books?

WILLA

But if Amazon didn't have the edition you needed?

HAL

I'd go to my favourite second-hand bookshop, on Charing Cross Road.

WILLA

Also not helpful, since I'm in LA.

HAL

Fine. If I really needed to find a specific edition of an old book, and I was in a hurry, do you want to know what I'd actually do?

WILLA

YES!

HAL

Go and find Alice and ask her in person.

WILLA

I'm already on my way.

ALICE

"The important thing to remember is that this is an *awareness* march," Darla told us all, from the front of the office. "So while our placards and posters can be fun and amusing, I also want them to be educational. I want the people who read them to *learn* something, and feel inspired to find out more. OK?"

A murmur of agreement went up through the room. I was sitting at the back, next to Jake, my hair across my face a little in case she realized I wasn't actually Willa – but to be honest, Jake's mum seemed far too busy preparing for the Save Our Seas march that weekend to care too much about one press-ganged volunteer.

"We've only got five days to get ready, and there's still a lot to do," she went on. "So, I'd like to run through the list if we can, to check who is dealing with what."

"What are we supposed to be dealing with?" I asked Jake in a whisper.

"Helping make placards, I think. Know any good

educational sea life puns?" He pulled a face.

"Live life on porpoise?" I suggested, remembering his T-shirt from the day we met.

"Seas the day?" he fired back, and I bit down on my cheek to keep from laughing.

As Darla ran through lists of responsibilities, I gazed around the room at all the dedicated Shore Thing volunteers. Then I frowned as something caught my eye.

"Is that Alice?" Jake murmured, indicating the window to the left of us, where Willa was waving madly through the glass, trying to get our attention. I felt a pang as he called her by my name, and I forced myself to slip back into character as Willa. Willa didn't find sea puns funny.

"Yep. I'd better go see what she wants." I slid from my seat as unobtrusively as possible and headed for the door. Jake followed.

"Finally!" Willa said as the door shut behind us. "You two were so engrossed in whatever is going on in there I thought you'd never notice me! What *is* going on in there, anyway? Movie afternoon? Donut-making demonstration? Live octopus dancing?"

"Plans for the awareness march on Saturday," I told her. I didn't even want to ask what live octopus dancing was. "What's the problem?" I glanced at Jake, hoping that it was something Willa could talk about in front of him.

"Uh…" She looked between us, and I could see she was trying to come up with a cover story for whatever it was. Then, apparently, she gave up. "I need to find a very specific 1980s edition of a Beatrix Frost novel and get it here by first thing tomorrow at the absolute latest."

I blinked. "Of course you do."

"Um, why?" I glanced across and saw that Jake had actually raised his hand to ask the question. It was kind of adorable. Except, I was trying to *not* find him adorable.

Willa glanced at me, presumably looking for help. I shrugged. I had nothing. Apart from anything else I had no idea of the *real* reason she needed some obscure book, so how could I come up with a fake reason?

"I, uh, so I made some new friends down at the beach, and they're filming a project for school and the book was one of the props. But someone – not me – accidentally tipped coffee all over it and now they need a replacement. They've already filmed a lot of the scenes with the book in, so it has to be exactly the same edition or the continuity will be off."

"Did you try Amazon?" Jake asked.

Willa gave him a withering stare.

"Right. OK. Do you have the original book?" I asked, thinking fast.

Pulling it from her bag, Willa handed me the sad, brown, coffee-stained paperback. I could just about make out where it said 'Beatrix Frost' on the front.

"We'll use the computers in the education suite," I said decisively. "Come on. If anyone can find this book, we can."

The problem, it turned out, with trying to find a forty-odd-year-old book, is that the remaining copies seemed to have travelled far and wide in the intervening decades.

"I've got one … in Japan," Jake said, after we'd all been searching online for a few minutes. I'd assumed that such a popular book would still be around in decent numbers, and it was. It was finding the right edition that was the problem. Several times I thought I'd found it only to realize that the cover was different, or it was a different format. Or in Japan. Or Paris. Or even Australia.

"This is hopeless." Willa slammed her mouse down on the desk and slumped back in her chair. "Nobody is going to be able to get one of these books to us in time for filming tomorrow – or even before we finish filming at the end of the week."

Jake and I exchanged a look. "You're really invested in this book thing, aren't you?" he said.

Willa seemed to realize that her cover story didn't fully explain her level of frustration. "I, uh, it's just that I promised to help. And I seriously hate letting people down." That, at least, sounded like something I might say.

"You're sure the film can't go on without it?" I asked.

"Positive." She sighed. "So now I'm going to have to go back in there and tell them I failed."

I winced on her behalf. Failure was not a thing that Willa Andrews allowed to happen to her. I knew how important this film was to her, and I wanted to help.

"Maybe we need to think more local," Jake said, snapping a photo of the book on his phone. "Hang on."

Moments later, my phone buzzed in my pocket. When I checked my notifications, it was a post from the Shore Thing Project, asking for help – and for people to share – the search for our book.

I raised my eyebrows. "Won't your mum mind you using the project's social media for your personal gain?"

"Hey, it's not for me. It's for Alice." He flashed me a smile. "And besides, why shouldn't we help people when we can, however we can?"

"Thanks, Jake." Willa's voice was smaller than usual. "I appreciate it."

I frowned, trying to catch a thought on the outskirts of my brain. "Something about local..." I muttered to myself.

"What?" Jake asked.

"Don't worry," Willa told him. "That's her thinking voice."

"Got it!" I grabbed my bag and pulled out my LA guidebook. "There's a bookshop I wanted to visit..." I fanned open the book and showed them the relevant page.

"An actual, old-fashioned bookstore," Jake said in amazement. "Why didn't we think of that?"

"I guess not everything has to be fixed by the internet," Willa replied with a shrug. "Come on, who's up for a road trip?"

The Last Bookstore, all the way in downtown LA, was my every book dream come to life. From the neon sign in the window of the old bank building to the rainbow bookshelves and book art inside, to the incredible book tunnel, all the way to Millie, the girl at the desk with the purple hair who helped us search the stacks.

We lost Jake to the incredible racks of vinyl records after a while, but Willa, Millie and I kept looking. We scoured bookcase after bookcase, from the classics aisles to the American Literature section to the boxes of newly donated books. Eventually, Willa threw herself into one of the red leather armchairs that were scattered around the giant building. But I kept searching.

"Is this it?" Millie held up a slightly battered but definitely-not-coffee-stained copy of Beatrix Frost's first novel, *Home from Eden*. Over in the corner, Willa sat bolt upright in her armchair and pulled the original book from her bag again. We held them together, comparing, until we were both satisfied.

"This is it," Willa said, sounding faintly astonished. "We did it."

"We did." I beamed at Millie. "Thank you so much!"

"All part of the service," Millie told us.

We paid for the book, then rounded up Jake (and his latest purchases) and headed back towards the metro.

"Will your friends still be filming when we get back?" Jake asked.

Willa checked my watch and shook her head. "They'll have called it for the day by now. But I can surprise them with this tomorrow!" She hugged the book close to her chest. "Thank you, both. I couldn't have done it without you."

"Oh, I don't know," I teased her. "I've never seen you not get what you want before, you know."

Willa grinned back. "That's true." Then she shot a meaningful look in Jake's direction. "We *both* seem to end up getting what we want when we're together, don't we?"

I glared at her. But I couldn't stop smiling all the same.

WILLA

I arrived at the agreed location on the Palisades the next morning feeling triumphant. It might have taken me all day – a full day of missed filming opportunities – but I had done the impossible. I'd found a non-coffee-stained perfect match for the book we needed. I was a hero.

For about twenty seconds.

I headed straight for Jenn when I arrived. She might not like me much – and I wasn't too fond of her either – but she'd been really upset the day before, so I thought she'd be thrilled I'd found the book.

"I got it!" I said, jogging up to her and waving the book around.

She snatched it from me, and instantly the sympathy I'd felt for her started draining away. "Great. Now maybe you can start pulling your weight around here again instead of hanging out with your mates. I'll go tell Fran that we've fixed the prop problem. You can take the coffee orders."

With that, she strode off with the book I'd spent

so many hours searching for and somehow I knew that by the time she reached Fran it wouldn't be *my* triumphant achievement she'd be talking about, or even *ours*. It would be all Jenn, and I'd just be the person who fetched coffee again.

And I was right. When Fran called us all together for our pre-shoot pep talk, Jenn was standing there beside her, smiling and holding the book.

"Our incredible Jenn has found us a replacement book!" announced Fran. Everyone whooped and cheered as if they'd forgotten that a) Jenn was the one who wrecked the book in the first place and b) *I* was the one who'd disappeared for a whole day to try to find a new one!

"We did lose a little time yesterday though," Fran went on. "Plus we still have all the beach scenes to film, so I think we're going to need to adjust the schedule and wrap the shoot on Saturday instead of Friday. Is that OK with everyone?" The tone of her voice suggested that this wasn't really a question. We all nodded, even though I wondered what the point was in me being there. Saturday was Alice's last full day, and the day of the Shore Thing Save Our Seas awareness march. Would they even notice if I wasn't there – apart from when they wanted their coffee?

But then again, I had to have that final 'it's a wrap' moment on film for my documentary. Which meant I had to be there to film it. And besides…

"That means we'll throw our wrap party on Saturday night instead, OK? Jenn, perhaps you can organize that for us, since you're so on fire this week. Willa can help."

Could I? Too right. If anyone knew how to throw a party, it was Willa Andrews. Jenn didn't look too pleased at the idea, but that was tough on her. I was going to throw the best party any of them had ever been to – and film it too.

That didn't mean I was any less mad with Jenn, though.

I confronted her, from the other side of the props trolley, once the others had gone to prep for today's shoot. "You didn't tell Fran it was me who found the book, did you?"

She shrugged. "I'm in charge of props. I have a new book to replace the old one. How that happened is basically irrelevant."

"Not to me."

Jenn sighed and looked up from the top tray of props to frown at me. "Willa, when are you going to realize that you're the least important person here?

No one cares where you were yesterday. Probably half of them didn't even notice you weren't there. It's not like you've been much help so far, anyway."

I gaped at her. I'd been loads of help! I'd shifted furniture, moved lights – and grumbled about it the whole time because I wanted to be filming my own stuff.

You're not a part of the team yet. Matty's words echoed around my head as Jenn stalked off, presumably to do something far more useful than I ever could.

He'd been right. They hadn't even noticed I wasn't there yesterday. I wasn't part of the team. *Yet.*

That was the word I had to focus on. I had five whole days to prove to the rest of them that I *was* part of the team. That I'd made a valuable contribution to the film – one worth mentioning in the credits, say, or to Mr Harris the film teacher, when he was choosing students for his special extra-credit class next year.

To prove to *myself* that this was something I could do, that I wanted to do.

Starting now.

Pushing my anger about Jenn and the book to one side, I took a breath, smiled, and went to see who I could help.

The rest of the day's filming went much better than the previous week, although how much of that was my shift in attitude and how much was just us getting into the swing of things, I couldn't be sure. But even Matty whispered a 'good job' to me after one particularly tricky scene finally went right – and I had lunch ready on hand for everyone to celebrate.

Fetching food and drink and shifting furniture might not seem like it mattered much in my filmmaker's education. But it *did* matter in teamwork, I realized. And everyone was much happier to film short interview segments for me too.

So, I was in a pretty good mood by the time I met Alice back at the Shore Thing.

"I've been thinking," she said as we switched clothes. "Now you're filming on the beach, we're more likely to both be around the Shore Thing at the same time, right? You said it would be easier for us to hang out, but that means more people might see us together. Do you think we'll be able to keep up the swap? I mean, maybe I should just tell Jake the truth. That would solve things, right?"

"Or we could just carry on like we've done for the last week, and be a little bit more careful when I'm here." I handed Alice her T-shirt. "Seems to me, the plan has been working pretty well. Unless you *want* to tell Jake..."

She sighed and sat down on the closed toilet seat. "I don't know. Maybe? I just... No. I mean, I'm Willa around him – I'm confident, I get on with stuff, I wear the sort of clothes I'd never dare wear at home... He likes Willa-me – albeit, Willa-me with Alice knowledge about the sea and climate change and stuff. Straight, boring Alice-me, probably not so much."

I shrugged. "Personally, I think he likes *you*, whatever your name is." Alice seemed to think that she was a completely different person when she was pretending to be me. All I saw was that she relaxed and let herself be the person she *wanted* to be the rest of the time.

"What do you think he'd say if you told him?" I asked. "I mean, would he want to make us tell the truth to everyone?" He seemed like a bit of a do-gooder, and the last thing I wanted was him making Alice feel so guilty that we had to come clean.

"I don't know." Alice sighed. "I don't think he'd tell anyone. But... No, it's better this way. Otherwise we'd have to say goodbye on Saturday, after the march. This way, he'll think I'm still in LA – like you

– and we might bump into each other or whatever, but it won't be a big deal."

"If you say so." Telling Jake or not telling Jake was up to Alice, I decided. I just had to trust her judgement on it. "Come on. We need to get going or Mum will come in looking for us."

Mum was the only person who absolutely knew the difference between us. And we'd managed to keep her away from everyone else since that very first day. Which is why my heart flew into my throat when we left the bathroom to find Mum coming out of Darla's office.

"Oh, this is not good," I whispered. Alice nodded, her eyes wide and terrified.

"Great! So Saturday it is. I'm so glad we were able to get something sorted," Mum was saying to Darla. "I know it's short notice, but sometimes that gives these events the most energy."

"Absolutely." Darla appeared in the doorway beside her and Alice ducked behind me. "And with the awareness march that afternoon, this should flow together perfectly. Thanks again, Sarra."

Mum shrugged. "Thank whichever network bigwig it was that said something stupid about climate change recently. My producer was desperate for a way to get some *positive* environmental publicity, and I just happened to be in the right place at the right time to make it happen."

"And thank you for lending us Willa this week too!" Darla went on, and Alice grabbed my hand tightly. "She's been an absolute godsend, helping Jake with everything. I don't know how we'd have managed without her."

Mum looked a little surprised at that. She knew I wasn't here by choice.

"Hi, Mum," I said, dragging Alice past them both at speed.

"Bye, Darla," Alice said as we left, which hopefully helped confuse the situation further.

Outside, we both made a beeline straight for the car.

"What do you think your mum was talking to Darla about?" Alice asked as we leaned against the hot metal, waiting for Mum to catch us up.

"No idea," I said with a shrug. "But I'm sure we'll find out soon enough."

Unfortunately, I was right.

ALICE

I'll be honest. Despite my curiousity, by the time Mrs Andrews got back to the car, I wasn't actually paying her much attention. Because all my thoughts were still caught up in my conversation with Willa in the bathroom.

About whether or not to tell Jake the truth.

I mean, I had definitely learned a few things pretending to be Willa last summer, and at least one or two of them were mistakes I didn't intend to make twice.

In particular: Luca.

Luca had been a brilliant friend to me the whole three weeks I spent in Italy. And when he discovered that I'd been lying to him the entire time ... it didn't go well.

I didn't want the same to happen with Jake.

Which gave me, I figured, two options. One: tell him the truth and hope he could be OK with it. Two: hope he never, ever found out, and never speak to him again after I left LA on Sunday.

When I looked at it like that, I really needed to tell him. Right?

But what if he hated me for lying anyway? Jake was a straightforward kind of person. And I didn't even have a great excuse this time, beyond 'Willa needed to be somewhere else, so I offered to cover for her.' He wasn't going to understand that being Willa gave me the chance to be a person I'd never have the courage to be on my own.

And that led me to my other fear. What if I *couldn't* be the same person once he knew the truth?

So that was what was filling my mind when Mrs Andrews started talking about some fundraiser on Saturday evening, after the march.

"Obviously Darla and her crew are going to be busy with the Save Our Seas march, but it really was the only day we could make it work, so I said that I'd take care of the setting up and supervising at the venue. Willa, Darla agreed that you could miss the march to help me with that."

That caught my attention. I'd worked hard on that march. No way I intended on missing it now.

But Mrs Andrews didn't want me, anyway, did she? She wanted Willa. And if I told Jake the truth, maybe no one else would notice if I was on the march…

Then I glanced over at Willa and saw the panic in her eyes, and realized it was going to be far more complicated than that.

We couldn't talk about it, of course, until we were in private again. But the moment we got home, even before Mrs Andrews pulled out the takeaway menus, we dashed straight upstairs to our bedroom to discuss.

"OK, I need you to be me on Saturday," Willa said, slamming the door behind her.

"I can't! I need to be on the march. *You* need to help your mum set up the fundraiser. There's no way she'll fall for me playing you anyway!"

"That's true." Willa stalked over to the window, pulling her hair up into a messy bun as she went – her usual plotting hairstyle. Except this time, there was nothing to plot. I was going on the march, she would help her mum, and we'd meet at the fundraiser afterwards. Easy.

Except Willa had to make it difficult. As usual.

"Well, we need to come up with something," she said, pacing back the length of the room again. "I need to be on set on Saturday for filming—"

"What? I thought you finished on Friday!" Saturday was supposed to be *our* day. We were going to go to the march together, then have a last night dinner and celebration. That second bit had already been ruined by the new fundraiser plans, but to know that Willa hadn't even intended to be there anyway … that hurt.

"We need an extra day," she said with a casual shrug, like she didn't even *remember* our plans. "We lost time over that book thing."

"The book thing that *I* fixed." My cheeks felt hot with frustration, but Willa didn't even seem to notice that I'd spoken at all.

"And I'm planning the wrap party for Saturday, so I definitely need to be there."

"But the fundraiser is that night!"

"I know. But there has to be some way we can make it work." She chewed on her bottom lip.

Inside me, I felt a new feeling swelling up. A certainty. A line I couldn't cross.

I was done.

"OK, I've got it." Willa bounced down on to her bed opposite me. "It's easy!"

"No," I whispered.

"Really, it is. We're going to be filming down at the beach on Saturday. So all you need to do is skip the march—"

"No." A little firmer this time, but Willa still didn't seem to notice.

"Then we *both* go and help Mum at the fundraiser, and whenever she asks us to do something—"

"I do it while you run off to your film?" I guessed.

"Exactly!"

"No."

This time, she heard me.

She stared at me in disbelief.

"Alice, I need you to do this. If I'm not there for the last day of filming, if I flake out on organizing the wrap party, the last two weeks will have been for nothing! I might as well have not been there at all."

"And imagine if you hadn't! You might actually have had to do your volunteering punishment yourself – and spend time with me! I came here to be with *you*, Willa, and instead you've just used me to cover for you, so you can run off and do what matters most to you – which definitely isn't our friendship."

Part of me could hardly believe I was saying these things, but part of me couldn't believe I hadn't said them sooner.

I'd offered to take Willa's place at the Shore Thing because I thought that pretending to be her would give me the confidence I seemed to have lost since last summer, and it had worked. Because the Alice who'd arrived in LA just over a week ago would never have had the confidence to say all this to Willa.

"Ha! You really think I wouldn't rather have been spending time with you this week?" Willa asked scornfully. "It was your idea to swap in the first place!"

"Only to help you! And right now I think I'd have been better off staying in London," I spat back.

Willa's smile turned sly. "Ah, but then you'd have never met Jake, would you? You can't fool me, Alice. I know how much you like him. You'd never have had the courage to flirt with him if you weren't pretending to be me. You should be thanking me for lending you my life!"

"I think the Shore Thing, and your mum, and everyone else should thank *me*. Because I've been a far better Willa for them this week than you would have been."

She stared at me. Regret welled up in me the moment the words were out of my mouth, but I couldn't take them back, not now. So I just stared back in silence.

"Girls! Dinner is here!" Mrs Andrews's voice echoed up the cavernous stairs of the mansion.

By the time we went to bed, backs turned towards each other in our huge beds, we still hadn't spoken another word to each other.

ALICE

Willa's not speaking to me.

ALICE

Actually, I'm not speaking to Willa.

ALICE

It's a mutual fury thing.

LUCA

What happened?

ALICE

We had a horrible argument and I said things I can't take back and she said stuff I don't think she even WANTS to take back and now it's just awful all the time.

ALICE

What should I do?

LUCA

The stuff you said ... did you mean it? Or are you sorry you said it now?

ALICE
Kind of both?

ALICE
I mean, I'm sorry I said it because I think it hurt her and things are horrible between us.

ALICE
But that doesn't mean the things I said weren't true.

LUCA
In that case ... I don't know. I mean, you can't say sorry for something you still mean.

ALICE
I know. That's why I'm just not saying anything at all.

WILLA

Things are kind of screwed up here.

WILLA

Alice and I had a fight.

HAL

You had a fight with ALICE? I didn't think she even knew HOW to argue.

WILLA

Apparently it's one of the many things she learned from being me.

HAL

Ah. That makes more sense. What did you argue about?

WILLA

Everything. She thinks I was just using her so I could work on the film this week.

HAL

Which is ... not entirely untrue, is it?

WILLA

But it's not like I PLANNED it this way. It just happened! If Mum hadn't volunteered me to do my punishment at the Shore Thing, or if Fran hadn't decided to film over the holidays, none of this would have happened.

HAL

Yeah, but you didn't have any control over those things. And you had other choices, right? You could have skipped the film and done your punishment with Alice. You CHOSE to do things this way.

WILLA

But Alice chose too! The whole plan was her idea, because she wanted to be me again. And she got to hang out with Hot Jake while I just fetched coffees and shifted furniture, so she kind of won the two weeks anyway!

HAL

Hot Jake?

WILLA

Um, that's not important. What matters is that Alice had a fun fortnight, whatever she's moaning about now. So why shouldn't she help me out and pretend to be me for Mum's fundraiser? I mean, yes, she'll have to miss the Save Our Seas march she was going to go on with Jake – but actually, she would only be there as me anyway! So if I'm not going, why should she?

HAL

Because maybe Alice wants to do something for herself, as herself, for a change? I'm just guessing.

WILLA

You're not making me feel any better about all this.

HAL

I'm not trying to.

WILLA

Alice still hadn't said another word to me by the time we reached the Shore Thing Project the next morning. Mum didn't seem to have noticed we weren't speaking, because she'd been talking non-stop about the fundraiser.

Here's what I'd learned about it:

It was being held at a really swanky hotel, just up from the Shore Thing offices.

The executive producer on Mum's show had invited all sorts of famous and/or rich people – basically everyone they knew – in the hope that *some* of them at least would be free at super short notice.

Darla was having to leave almost everything to Mum to arrange, because she had her hands full with the awareness march – but that was OK, because Mum was in her element anyway.

Mum was calling in favours from her favourite designers to borrow dresses for her, Alice and me to wear.

Getting ready for the fundraiser was totally going

to clash with Alice's march and my filming, and the fundraiser itself would be at exactly the same time as the wrap party for the film, which completely sucked.

My life was a disaster.

I left Alice at the Shore Thing and headed down to the beach, where we were filming. At least now we were both working vaguely in the same place I didn't have to dash back across town again. In fact, if Alice and I were friends, I could probably have nipped back up to meet her for lunch. Or she could have come and visited our set down on the beach.

As it was, I just concentrated on being useful to Fran and the others, and filming when I could. It was weird, but I somehow seemed to have more time and opportunities to film my own stuff when I was putting *more* effort into doing what the others needed.

"What's the most important thing you've learned while working on this film?" I asked Kat as Derek applied her make-up. I'd been asking everyone on the cast and crew the same question, and it was interesting hearing all their different answers.

It had made me start to think a bit about what *I'd* learned too.

Kat considered the question for a few moments as Derek feathered mascara on to her lashes. "I guess the main thing is … how much we can all achieve when we work together," she said at last. "I mean, we're all still students, right? But I think we're going to be really proud of this film by the end."

I smiled at her as I lowered my camera. "Me too."

"Plus you'll have a *much* better technique for a good smokey eye," Derek added, making us both laugh.

By the end of the day's shoot, I was tired, sandy and a little bit sunburned across my shoulders. But I had a good feeling about the film, at last – even if everything else still seemed to be falling apart. At least I'd got *something* right this spring break.

I was just helping to pack up the equipment – making very sure that no sand had got somewhere it shouldn't along the way – when I found Jenn.

The trolley she'd been using to store the props didn't work so well on sand, so she'd been toting them around in a giant holdall all day. Now, she was sat on the sand, tears of frustration leaking from her eyes as she stared down at the bag. I followed her gaze and saw that the strap had snapped.

"Need a hand carrying that somewhere?" I guessed that Matty had brought his car, so it shouldn't be too far to lug it. Between us, it was totally manageable.

But Jenn looked at me as if I'd lost my mind. "Why would *you* help me?"

Actually, that was a good question. She'd been pretty horrible to me since the start of filming, and I'd returned the favour. But over the last couple of days I'd learned that a willingness to help went a long way towards making life more pleasant.

"Look, Jenn, I know we didn't exactly get off to a great start, but we're all working together on this film, right? So let me help you with the bag."

Determination etched on to her face, Jenn struggled to her feet and hoisted the bag into her arms. It looked like she was going to struggle to make it even a few metres up the beach, but it was clear there was no way she was letting me help her.

Shrugging, I turned my back and headed towards where the others were still packing up. Until I heard a *whumph* of something heavy hitting the sand and turned to find Jenn flat on her back.

"OK, *now* will you let me help? Or let me go fetch Matty to help you, if you don't want me to do it."

"No!" Panic flared in Jenn's eyes.

"No to me helping or no to getting Matty?" I asked, confused.

"Both. But especially … don't get Matty."

OK, there was definitely something going on here.

Crouching down on the sand next to Jenn, I asked, "Why not? I mean, he's your boyfriend. He'll want to help you, right?"

"And that's exactly why." With a sigh, Jenn unzipped the holdall and, fishing out another, smaller bag, started moving some of the props from the big bag to the empty one. "I know what everyone is saying about me."

"What's that?"

"That I'm only on the crew because I'm going out with Matty and he begged Fran to let me help out somehow. That I'm jealous of the two of them. That I wasn't interested in film at all before we got together, and I'm only pretending to be interested now so I can keep an eye on him. That I'm not really committed to the production." The last one she said in a whisper, like it was a terrible, terrible secret.

I thought about what she'd said, and frowned. "Yeah, but, *I'm* only on the crew because Matty begged Fran to let me help. And if they were going to accuse anyone of not being committed…" I winced. "Up until this week it would definitely have been me, right?"

Jenn glanced at me and I saw the ghost of a smile cross her lips. "Well, yeah. But Matty raved about your talent, told Fran she had to let you on because you'd be an asset to the film. Nobody thinks it's because you don't have enough talent to get there on your own, or because you can't trust your boyfriend."

"Talent isn't everything though, is it?" I said ruefully. "I mean, however good you are, if you can't work as part of a team you're not going to get far on a film set."

"That's true." Jenn looked a little more hopeful, suddenly. "And I *am* good at teamwork."

"Well, apart from when you're stealing the credit for someone else's miraculous book find," I reminded her.

"Yeah. I'm sorry about that. I just… I screwed up, you know? So I felt like *I* needed to fix it."

"I can understand that, I guess." I sat next to her, stretching my legs out on the sand. "So why *did* you want to be on the film, if it wasn't because of Matty?"

Jenn shrugged, staring out at the ocean as she answered. "I've always loved movies. They were something I learned about with my dad, before he left. We'd watch old movies and he'd tell me all about the behind-the-scenes gossip and stuff. He used to work as a cameraman at one of the big studios, you see, and he'd let me make mini-movies with his personal camera at home on weekends. I'd get my friends to act them out for me."

"Sounds fun."

"It was. We used to test each other on past Oscar winners."

I raised an eyebrow. That was a game I could play too. "Oh really? Best Picture, 1935?"

Jenn didn't miss a beat. "*It Happened One Night*. First film to scoop all of the big five academy awards."

"And my favourite film of all time. Huh. I guess you really do love movies. So, what happened?"

She sighed. "My dad left. And I was so angry with him… I guess I shut out all the parts of my life that I associated with him. I didn't even go to the movies for three whole years. It was only when I started dating Matty that I remembered how much I'd loved film, and wanted to get involved again. So I asked him to get me on this shoot."

"I made my best friend pretend to be me and take my volunteer punishment at an ocean conservation charity this spring break so I could be here." The words blurted out of me unprompted. I definitely hadn't *meant* to tell Jenn, but she was sharing her story and I guess I felt like I had to give something back. Plus she knew my favourite movie. That counted for something, right?

She looked up at me, obviously astonished. "You mean Alice? The girl from London we met at your house?"

I nodded.

"She came all this way to see you, and you sent her to volunteer at some ocean project?"

"OK, when you put it like that it sounds really bad."

"Willa!" Jenn kneeled up on the sand and stared at me. "It *is* bad."

I buried my head in my hands. "I know. I know it is. And now she's not speaking to me because I wanted her to miss an awareness march she cares about to cover for me, so I could be here for the last day of filming and the wrap party on Saturday."

"Oh. The wrap party." The amazement was gone from Jenn's voice. I peeked through my fingers and saw that she'd sunk back down on her heels, looking despondent again.

"OK, so I know we still need to do some work to get the party sorted, but you have the venue arranged, right?" I asked. "You said you knew someone who could get us a space?"

I'd been happy to leave that part to Jenn. It wasn't exactly like we had a budget for this party, beyond what was left from the costumes and props fund, so we'd take any freebies we could get.

"Yeah. I know. But … it didn't work out. So I've been calling around *everywhere* and still nothing. Everywhere is either booked or wants a huge deposit and I can't give them that." Poor Jenn sounded so downhearted I genuinely felt sorry for her.

"We'll find somewhere," I said with a shrug. "I mean, the party is all of us being together, celebrating the end of the film, right? So the where isn't nearly as important as the why."

"I suppose," Jenn said, not sounding entirely convinced. "I just really wanted to show them all that it was worth having me on the project."

"Trust me," I told her. "If we work together, we can pull it off. It'll be the best wrap party ever."

ALICE

I'd been practising what I wanted to say to Jake all morning in my head. It was a nice distraction from the fact that Willa wouldn't even look at me over breakfast, then put her headphones on the minute we got on the bus to Santa Monica so she didn't have to talk to me.

Which was fine, because I wasn't talking to her anyway. In fact, I'd kind of lost track of which one of us was more mad at the other. But I had decided one thing, somewhere in the middle of our argument.

I needed to tell Jake the truth.

I found him assembling placards in the education suite.

"Hey, Willa! Great. Can you hold this in place while I tape it on?" His easy smile made my insides twinge with guilt. Still, I held the sign like he'd asked, and tried to remember the final script I'd decided on.

"Great news about the fundraiser your mom's

arranging." Jake placed a long piece of tape across the stick and stuck it in place on the board. "Does it mean I'll get to see you in a glamorous gown or something?" He flashed me a grin. "Although, to be honest, I think I probably prefer you in your jean shorts and tees. Much more practical for going kayaking."

He was flirting with me. Actually flirting with me. And I liked it. I liked *him*.

Which was just another reason I had to tell him the truth.

I swallowed, my mouth dry. "Jake. I need to tell you something."

His smile turned a little sad. "Don't worry. Mom already told me that you'd have to miss the march to help your mom set up. And I totally understand. It's just a shame for you, because you've put so much into it. And obviously we'll miss having you there, but we can catch up at the fundraiser later, right?"

I shook my head. "That's not it. Not all of it, anyway. Because the thing is… I won't be helping get ready for the fundraiser. Because Willa will. I hope. So I can still be on the march because I'm not Willa."

Did that even make any sense?

A confused frown settled on to Jake's forehead, suggesting it didn't. "You're not… Wait, what?"

I sank into the nearest chair and prepared to explain the whole thing.

"When Willa and I first met last summer, we were on a plane to London and neither of us wanted to go where we were supposed to be going, so we swapped places."

"Mom told me that story," Jake said. "I wasn't even sure I believed it."

"And now, this spring break, Willa had plans to be involved in a student movie project and I liked the idea of being here, so it sort of made sense for us to swap again. Somehow."

"So you're *Alice*. Not Willa. Willa's friend. But Mom and I met you *both* that first day. I've seen Alice – I mean, Willa – most days too. And Mrs Andrews has been dropping you off and picking you up... How could we not know?"

I gave him a faint smile. "It's pretty easy to make assumptions, I guess. Apart from Willa's mum, no one knew either of us well enough to distinguish which of us was which. And when I'm wearing Willa's clothes and she's in mine, people just assume we are who we say we are."

Jake shook his head. "I just... Why? I don't understand. Why did you swap?"

"I told you. Willa had this film project commitment—"

"No, no, I get why *Willa* wanted to trade places. But why did *you*, Alice?"

It sounded so weird to hear him call me by my actual name. But I had to admit, it sounded good in his Californian accent.

"I guess … partly it was because I knew how much this film meant to Willa." Even though thinking about it now made me cross with her all over again, at the start, I had genuinely wanted to help her. I just hadn't realized how much advantage she'd take of that. "But then, I wanted to be here for *me* too."

"Because you care about ocean conservation?" Jake asked doubtfully, but with a hint of hope.

"Definitely," I assured him. "My dad's a marine biologist working in conservation. I honestly care about this stuff – far more than Willa would have!"

Jake looked relieved. "I was worried that was all part of the act too," he admitted.

"No. Not at all." I shook my head emphatically, in case my words weren't enough. "In fact, if Willa had needed to volunteer anywhere else, I might not have suggested it!"

Jake must have seen some uncertainty in my face,

because he asked, "What else? What else made you say yes to this?"

"Last summer, when Willa and I first swapped places … I got to let go of being *Alice*. Because Alice is nothing like Willa, really, and I kind of needed to be someone else for a while back then."

"So you've been acting like another person the whole time I've known you?" Jake asked. "Not just swapping your names, but actually playing a part, like an actor?" I could hear the hurt in his voice.

"That's the strange thing," I told him. "I thought I'd be happier if I acted more like Willa again. But in fact, I've been more *myself* here with you these last ten days, than I've felt in ages."

"I'm glad. Because I really like the girl I got to know this holiday."

"You know, I think I quite like her too," I joked. Then my voice turned more serious. "And you. I've really liked spending time with you, Jake. And I'm sorry that I lied to you."

"Yeah. So am I."

"What are you thinking?" I asked warily.

"I don't know," he admitted. "Just … trying to get my head around it all, I guess. It feels like I've wasted time, getting to know someone who doesn't even exist."

"But I *do* exist! Like I said, I've been more me than Willa all along."

"Yeah." He looked up and met my gaze. "But Willa Andrews lives in LA, doesn't she? And you…"

I got there without him needing to finish the sentence. "I live in London. Yeah."

We looked at each other in silence for a moment.

"When do you go back?" Jake asked eventually.

"Sunday. The day after the march."

"Right."

This was why I shouldn't have told him. No, why I shouldn't have let myself get close to him in the first place. Because I was going to have to say goodbye, soon, and that would hurt.

"Then I guess we'd better make the most of the time we have left, hadn't we?" Jake said. But his smile didn't quite reach his eyes.

WILLA

I knew I needed to find a way to make up with Alice. Not to convince her to cover for me at the fundraiser, but because of my conversation with Jenn. She was right about the importance of being part of a team – and Alice and me had always been our *own* team. Until now.

And I missed it. I missed her.

I'd wasted so much of Alice's visit already – not just with the filming, but in time spent arguing and not speaking to each other. But I knew just saying sorry and expecting things to go back to normal wasn't good enough. I had to figure out a way to make sure she got to go on her march. Preferably one that also fixed my issues with the fundraiser and wrap party clash too.

Anyway, I was still mulling over my dilemma as I sat out on the deck at the Shore Thing Project, waiting for Alice to finish whatever it was she was working on today. Guilt pangs ate at my stomach again as I realized I barely even knew what she'd been doing here – what *I* was supposed to have been doing here. I had a horrible feeling I might have really messed up this spring break. I just hoped it wouldn't screw up my friendship with Alice forever too.

"Willa."

I started at the sound of my name and turned to find Jake walking out on to the deck, coming towards me. I was so surprised to see him without Alice, that it took me a moment to realize what he'd called me.

Willa. Not Alice.

"Alice told you," I guessed.

"She did."

Jake sat down beside me, his legs dangling off the edge of the deck like mine.

"Are you…" *Going to tell your mum? Going to tell* my *mum? Or Principal Carter?* "…mad?" I finished, after a short pause.

"With Alice? Not really. It's a lot to come to terms with – especially the part where it turns out the girl I've spent the last week falling for is leaving the country on Sunday. But I understand why she did it, I think."

"So you're mad with me." An easy assumption to make.

"I think Alice has that covered for both of us, don't you?" He looked sideways at me as he spoke.

I sighed. "Definitely. And I want to make it up to her, I do! I just … I want to find a way to make it right for *everybody*." And that, I realized, included the Shore Thing Project.

The ironic thing was that I *did* care about our oceans. I loved Santa Monica beach and I wanted it to stay beautiful forever, and to clean up the parts that were kind of yucky. I'd just chosen what *I* wanted over what others needed. As usual.

"I need a new plan," I said firmly.

"Well, if you really want to make amends, sorry is always a good place to start," Jake said. "Besides, if it's a plan you're after, I happen to know a girl who's great at organizing stuff. You might have met her. Beautiful, smart, confident … goes by the name of Alice. Well, usually, anyway."

I laughed despite myself. "I can see why she likes you. You see her the way I do."

Jake's face broke into a wide grin. "In that case, why don't you go make up with her fast so she can stop moping, then I can ask her to be my date to the fundraiser on Saturday, and we can make the most of our last few days together."

"It's a deal. Where is she?" I got to my feet, brushing sand from my legs.

"Where else? The education suite."

"Of course. Thanks, Jake."

He looked up at me, squinting in the sunlight. "You're welcome. Just don't screw it up."

"I'll try," I promised. And then I went to find Alice.

ALICE

"Alice?"

I looked up at the sound of Willa's voice.

"I just wanted to say … I'm sorry." Willa stayed in the doorway, like she wasn't sure if she'd be welcome inside or not. "You were right. I took advantage of you being here to get what I wanted and I didn't really think much about what *you* wanted. But I am thinking about it now, I promise."

"Really?" I raised my eyebrows a little. "So that means I can go on the march and *you'll* actually help your mum with the fundraiser set-up?"

"Yes to the march," she said with a small, tight smile. "I'm still working on the other part."

She'd said sorry. That counted for a lot. And she seemed to understand that the awareness march really did matter to me – as much as the film project mattered to her.

Which reminded me.

"I'm sorry too." The words whooshed out of me and I felt better almost instantly. I really don't like arguing with *anybody,* let alone my best friend. "Swapping was my idea in the first place and I shouldn't have said such awful things to you."

Willa's smile became more genuine and she moved into the room, hopping up on to one of the tables. She stared down at her feet as she said, "Actually, I think you probably should. I get an idea in my head and I just go for it but I don't always think about how it affects other people. The thing is, I want to get better." Willa looked up and met my gaze with her own fierce, determined one. "I want to think about others instead of myself – well, at least *as well* as myself. Starting with this fundraiser."

My eyebrows went up at that. "Really? You *want* to help with your mum's fundraiser?"

"I want to help the Shore Thing Project," Willa said. "I do actually care about our oceans too, you know."

"I know. I just didn't think—" I broke off.

But Willa finished the thought for me. "You didn't think I cared about them more than I cared for myself."

"Well…" I squirmed uncomfortably and focused on the leaflets in my hand.

"It's OK," Willa said. "I didn't. Probably still don't, to be honest. But I'm *trying.* And I hope that counts for something."

"It does," I assured her. "It counts for a lot."

"Good. Because I need your help to do it."

"To … care for the oceans?" I asked, confused.

Willa rolled her eyes at me. "To come up with a plan!"

"A plan to help with the fundraiser?"

"A plan to be in three places at once," she corrected, a wicked smile on her face.

I returned it, relief flooding through me as I realized our friendship was back on track.

"So you want to help the Shore Thing Project *and* get exactly what you want?" I summarized. Yep, that was Willa all right.

"And get you what *you* want!" she pointed out defensively. "Here's what we need: a plan that means you can go on the awareness march, I can help with the last day of filming, Mum pulls off a fantastic fundraiser to impress her producer and his fancy guests, the Shore Thing gets more donations, support and people caring about the oceans, and my film cast and crew get an awesome wrap party they won't forget. Oh, and you get to dress up in a designer gown and go on a date with Jake."

"What?" I asked, startled.

"He's going to ask you to the fundraiser," Willa

said slowly as if speaking to someone whose grasp of English was kind of limited. "You are absolutely going to say yes."

"Am I?"

I liked him. A lot. And even if I had to say goodbye really soon, I guess that didn't mean we shouldn't enjoy the time we had left together.

"You are!" Willa said, but it wasn't an instruction this time. It was a delighted realization.

"I think I am," I said, grinning. "But first, we have to come up with a plan to fix the whole list of problems."

Willa nodded, all business again. "So. Awareness march, filming, wrap party and fundraiser. OK, so that's four places in one afternoon and evening, and there's still only two of us. Plus, Mum has to think we're both at the fundraiser at all times. What do you think? Impossible?"

WILLA

I apologized to Alice.

HAL

Good.

WILLA

She apologized to me too.

HAL

Even better.

WILLA

So now we're coming up with the plan to end all plans that can have us in four places at once without anyone noticing we're not both where we're supposed to be, and while also raising a lot of money for a good cause. Hopefully.

HAL

And this message thread was going so well...

WILLA

Have faith. Anyway, it's not going to be my plan this time. It's Alice's.

HAL

Wait. Wasn't the *last* one Alice's too?

WILLA

Um. Yeah. OK, scratch that last bit.

WILLA

It took a whole pad of Post-it Notes, but eventually we had a plan.

"What happened in here?" Jake asked, bafflement on his face as he stared at the line of placards for the march, all now covered in bright pink, yellow, green and blue Post-it Notes. He turned to me. "I thought you were just going to apologize."

"And come up with a plan," I reminded him. I waved a hand towards the Post-it Notes. "This is the plan."

"I've almost got it." Alice turned towards us, chewing thoughtfully on her lower lip. "But it's going to take a lot of help from a lot of people."

"Then we just have to convince them it'll be worthwhile," I said, with a bit more confidence than I actually felt.

"How?" Alice asked.

"It's easy. Watch." I turned to Jake. "If you help us pull this off, not only will the Shore Thing raise a lot of money *and* awareness, but you'll definitely get a date with Alice on Saturday night."

Jake shrugged. "I'm in."

"See?" I told Alice. "Easy."

"I'm not sure everyone on these notes will be so easy to convince," Alice said, her gaze straying back to her colour-coded strategy. Seriously. That girl would colour-code the world if other people would just get on board with her plan.

But then I looked at all the names written in Alice's precise handwriting and realized she had a point.

"Well. We won't know until we ask," I said. "Let's figure out who is going to talk to who."

The next morning, we were ready to put our plan into action.

Alice and Jake were dealing with the people at the Shore Thing, and everything connected to the awareness march. Which left me with my guys at the film project, and the swanky hotel where Mum had booked the fundraiser.

After our heart-to-heart the day before, I decided to start with Jenn.

"**What would you say if I told you I could solve all your problems in one day?**" Best to go in bold, I'd decided.

"I'd ask you what the catch is," Jenn replied, not even looking up from where she was lining up the props needed for the morning's filming.

"So young, so cynical," I lamented. "The catch, as ever, is that you have to work for it."

That made her look at me. "I *always* work for things."

"Then this shouldn't be a problem, should it?" I smiled my sweetest smile, which only caused her to sigh.

"So basically, you need me to do something for you, and you're trying to pretend it's actually for me?"

I shook my head. "Not at all. I need you to help me convince a lot of people to do a lot of things: help save the planet, make a real difference, and give us somewhere to throw the wrap party."

"You found somewhere to host the party?" Jenn asked, genuine excitement in her voice at last.

Not the part Alice had hoped people would focus on, but I'd take it. "Yep. But like I said, we'll need to work for it."

Jenn met my gaze head on. "Tell me what I need to do."

As it turned out, getting Jenn on board was the easy part. Once I'd briefed her on the finer details of our plan, we had to convince the rest of the cast and crew.

Fran, inevitably, was the hardest to talk round, but I needed her buy-in to make it happen at all, so we started there.

"I just don't think we have the time," she said, after we'd explained. "I mean, it's not like I don't agree with what you're trying to achieve here, Willa. But this is our senior project. It's a big deal."

"Unlike, say, protecting our oceans?" I wasn't above a bit of guilt-tripping, if that's what worked, and I knew for a fact that Fran cared a *lot* about environmental issues. The war between ethics and good grades was playing out on her face.

"We can't risk not finishing the film on time," she warned.

"We'll finish on time." Hopefully. "Look, I've managed to film my behind-the-scenes project alongside everything else, right? So I'll put that to one side and do this now instead. It'll hardly take any time at all, and we're filming here at Santa Monica beach this week anyway. You guys are all such pros, it'll be quick work, and we'll just organize it around the filming schedule. It'll be fine."

"And you really think you can pull off the wrap party too?" Fran asked, not sounding entirely convinced.

"Absolutely!" I lied. I shared a quick look with Jenn.

"Well, with a little help from my friends."

Fran hesitated, indecision clear on her face. Then she nodded. "OK. You can ask the rest of the team. But I'm not telling anyone they *have* to take part. You'll have to convince them to do the extra work."

"Easy," I said, with more confidence than I felt.

"How are we going to do this?" Jenn asked in a whisper as Fran walked away to start blocking the next scene with Polly and Bethany.

I considered the question. "Well. Let's start by going and getting everyone coffee. They're always in a better mood when they're caffeinated."

"Good plan," Jenn agreed, so we headed for the nearest coffee shop.

One small step at a time, that was how we were going to do this.

"Phase one complete," I told Alice when I met her at the Shore Thing later that afternoon. "I got everyone on board. Eventually." Lara on the sound desk had been a bit of a hold-out, but once everyone else agreed she'd rolled her eyes, taken a long sip of her iced caramel latte and said yes. "How about here?"

"All on target," Alice replied, sounding a little

smug. "Jake and I spoke with all the volunteers and they think it's a great plan – and they promised to keep it a surprise for his mum too."

"You didn't mention the—"

"No! No, that's still a surprise for *everyone*. And speaking of which, now we just need to get things organized at the hotel…"

"Leave that one to me."

After dealing with Fran, convincing the hotel was actually surprisingly easy. Mum met us at the Shore Thing as usual but instead of heading straight home, the three of us visited the Oceanside Hotel to confirm all the arrangements for the fundraiser. While Alice kept Mum busy choosing colour schemes (navy blue, sea green and silver), decorations, and the room layout, I had a quiet word with the event planner about our more unusual requirements.

"It's supposed to be a surprise," I told her in a low voice. "You know, the real showstopper moment of the event. We don't even want the Shore Thing Project representatives to know in advance. Makes their reaction more real on film, you know?"

This was an LA hotel, so as I'd hoped, Amy the event planner just nodded and smiled agreeably when I handed her the printed sheet of the extras we needed to add in. Making things look real on film was basically this city's reason for being.

"I think we've decided!" Mum said, and soon we were done.

Now we just had twenty-four hours to put everything else in place for Saturday night.

How hard could it be?

ALICE

"I think Jake would like the silver one." Lounging across the loveseat in Mrs Andrews' room-sized closet – something I didn't know bedrooms could even have – Willa waved a random shoe at the silky dress hanging on the rail.

Mrs Andrews looked round from her own rail of dresses. "What matters most is that you're comfortable in it, Alice. Don't let my daughter talk you into something you're going to regret later."

Willa and I exchanged an amused look. "Too late for that," I mouthed at her.

I was pretty sure I *would* regret the silver dress. It was beautiful but I knew I'd spend all night fiddling with the straps and worrying they were going to fall down. Plus, the shoes the stylist had put with it were far too high for me to walk in without breaking an ankle.

It was a Willa dress. And as much fun as I'd had playing Willa this holiday, I wanted to go to this fundraiser as Alice.

"You take it. I think I like the bluey-green one," I decided, lifting it from the hanger again. "What do you think?"

Willa and Mrs Andrews stood next to each other, looking weirdly alike as they both tilted their heads to study my choice.

"I think it's perfect," Mrs Andrews said decisively.

"Very you," Willa added with a smirk.

The dress I'd picked – which the stylist had described as 'sea foam' in colour – was long and flowy and felt more like a princess dress than anything I'd ever owned before. It fit me perfectly, like it had been made for me. I silently thanked whichever celeb had turned it down, which had led to it being brought over to the house.

"Then I think we're all decided!" Mrs Andrews said, clapping her hands. "I'll wear the navy with the silver trim, *Willa* will wear the silver and Alice the sea foam. Perfect!"

Now there was nothing to do now but wait, and hope all our plans fell into place.

WILLA

I've never been any good at waiting. Fortunately I had enough work left to do to distract me that night, before the action the next day.

"Is it going to be ready in time?" Alice asked, hovering nervously at my shoulder as I focused on the screen.

"One way or another," I told her.

Editing footage is one of my favourite things to do. I mean, I love the rush of capturing all those moments that will never happen exactly the same way again. But taking hours of film and choosing the perfect bits to piece together to tell the story I want to share? That is so satisfying.

Or it would have been, if Alice's shadow wasn't covering my screen.

"Are you sure?" she asked.

"I'm sure it would go a lot quicker if you stopped hovering," I told her, smiling to show that I was joking. Mostly.

Alice took the hint and flopped on to her bed with

her phone in her hands.

"Hal wants to know how it's going," she said. "And Luca wishes us both good luck for tomorrow."

"We don't need luck," I said confidently. "We have a perfect plan."

There was no answer to that, and when I looked back Alice had her eyebrows raised at me over the top of her phone.

"We do!" I told her. "You worry too much."

"I worry just the correct amount to make sure everything goes perfectly," Alice said primly, then laughed at herself. "I mean, *one* of us has to worry, right?"

"And it isn't going to be me, because I know everything is going to go exactly to plan." After all, it was Alice's plan, and she always triple-checked everything.

Still, it wouldn't hurt to do a little checking myself. I fired off a few messages to the rest of the cast and crew while I waited for some files to upload. Matty and I were already in contact online, sending bits of film back and forth to check over.

Things were coming together.

"Everyone still on board?" Alice asked as my phone pinged with return messages.

"Of course they are," I said as if I'd never doubted it for a moment.

The only thing that worried me about this plan was how many people it involved. I mean, last summer, the only people who really counted were me and Alice. No one else even knew what was happening – well, until I met Hal, but he was easy enough to get onside.

This time … there were so many people who could change their minds or screw up somehow. We just had to trust that they wouldn't.

And now I was letting Alice's anxieties get to me. I shook them away and focused on the film again.

"Can you believe that this is nearly over?" Alice said suddenly. "That this time tomorrow I'll be packing to go back to London?"

"No." Sadness settled on my shoulders for a second. The two weeks of Alice's visit had flown by so fast, and I knew we hadn't used them as best as we could. Next time, I promised myself, I'd make sure that every moment we had together was fun. Next time.

"It's gone really quickly," Alice went on, and I nodded.

"Too quickly."

She shot me a sympathetic smile. "Well, at least

we've still got one last hurrah tomorrow."

I grinned. "We most definitely have."

As long as I finished this film on time.

Back to work. I'd worry about tomorrow, tomorrow.

ALICE

The next morning, Willa and I ran through the plan one last time, mostly to calm my nerves.

The day was warming up already. I dressed in my denim shorts and a Shore Thing Project T-shirt that Jake had given me, and picked up the dress bag that Mrs Andrews had packed my fundraiser outfit in, before heading down for breakfast. Willa, dressed in an almost identical outfit, was already downstairs making waffles.

"Are you sure you two will be OK on the march on your own?" Mrs Andrews asked as I smothered my waffle in chocolate sauce.

"Darla and Jake will be there, Mum," Willa reminded her. "We'll be fine."

"And you'll both definitely be at the hotel by three to help me set up?" I think the stress of organizing the fundraiser was starting to get to her. She'd never shown this much concern about our movements until now.

"Absolutely," I promised. "I've put an alarm on my phone and everything."

Mrs Andrews smiled fondly at me. "Thank you, Alice. If it was just Willa, I'd worry, but with you there I'm sure everything will be fine. And I'm sorry you'll have to miss some of the march, but hopefully the fundraiser will make up for it."

"I'm sure it will."

That had been the compromise part of the plan. I mean, I was good at planning, but even I'm not four-places-at-once good. But I'd managed to work it so that I'd be there for the most important parts of the march, and Willa would be where she needed to be too, and we'd *both* be at the actual fundraiser when it mattered.

"Right, well I'll see you girls later!" Grabbing her reusable bamboo coffee cup, Mrs Andrews swept out of the house and headed off to the studio for the morning.

As the door crashed shut behind her, Willa turned to me. "How come she trusts you so much more than me, her own actual daughter?"

I shrugged. "I'm the good one."

That made her laugh. "Sometimes I think I'm the only one who sees you as you actually are, you know."

"Maybe," I agreed. "But you have to admit, it does come in useful."

"Very." Willa shoved the last of her waffle into her mouth. "Come on. We've got a lot to do this morning."

We stashed our dresses at the hotel for later, and Willa checked in one last time with the event planner, then we went our separate ways: me to the march, and Willa down to the beach for the last day of filming.

Jake was waiting for me when I made it to the assigned meeting place. I recognized a lot of the Shore Thing volunteers already standing around in T-shirts like mine, holding some of the placards Jake and I had spent the week making.

Every volunteer got a handful of leaflets to give out as we marched. The hope was that we'd pick up more people to join us along the way – and the social-media campaign Jake and I had run over the last couple of weeks seemed to have brought out quite a few locals to march with us too.

"How long can you stay?" Jake asked as we prepared to start walking.

"I think I'll peel off when we pass the Oceanside Hotel," I said. "I need to go and get changed, as well as helping Willa's mum. But I'll definitely be back in time for the big finale."

He grinned. "Couldn't miss that now, could we?"

"Nope!" As long as everything went to plan…

Nerves jangled through me as we started to line up. A small LAPD contingent was there to make sure everything stayed peaceful and no one got hurt during the march. Someone was playing music with a water theme, interspersed with whale song. It was thematically great, but I couldn't help but think the short bits of waterfalls and rivers in between tracks were going to make everyone need the loo all afternoon.

At the front of the crowd Darla climbed up on to a bench to make a short speech of welcome and encouragement, which went down well – but then, the crowd we'd gathered were so enthusiastic about our cause I reckoned she could have just held up pictures of jellyfish and they'd have cheered.

It was something else, being surrounded by so many people who cared about the same things I did. The buzz of excitement and possibility that hummed through the group set me grinning – and even made me forget about all the things that could still go wrong.

"We're here today to make a difference!" Darla

shouted, and everyone cheered. "I want the whole of this city to know exactly why these oceans matter, and what they can do to help save them. So let's get out there and show them!"

At her words, the crowd started to move forwards, still cheering and shouting and laughing and chatting. Jake and I moved with them, and suddenly we were marching to Save Our Seas.

My whole body seemed to vibrate with the thumping of feet on the pavement and the excitement that filled the air.

I was so caught up in the feeling of being part of something that *mattered*, I almost forgot to slip out when we reached the Oceanfront Hotel.

"Your stop," Jake said, nudging my arm to remind me. "You'll catch us up later?"

I nodded. "Definitely."

"Then I'll see you there." And then, just as I was about to turn and go, he leaned down and pressed a swift kiss to the corner of my mouth.

Before I could even react, the crowd had swept him along, still singing and calling out chants as they marched, leaving me at the side of the road, stunned.

Then my phone beeped to remind me of the time.

I took a deep breath, blinked a few times and ran to the hotel.

I'd think about Jake, and that almost kiss, later.

Right now, I had a plan to put into action.

WILLA

"Will you stop bouncing around like that?" Jenn snapped, around mid-morning. "You're making *me* nervous."

"I just... What if we don't finish filming in time?" I asked, shifting from foot to foot on the sand.

This was the part of the plan neither Alice nor I had any control over. Fran had only agreed to my plan in the first place if it didn't interfere with finishing the film. And it *shouldn't*, as long as we didn't run over with the filming.

Since the final scene took place on the beach, and that was where we were filming on our last day anyway, Fran had decided to save it for last. Except now Finn kept fluffing his lines, and the one time he got them right Derek suddenly realized that Kat's costume was wrong for continuity from the last scene, so he had to fix that before they started over ... and now we were running late.

"Look, you've got the film for tonight all sorted, right?" Jenn said.

I nodded. It had taken me until midnight the night before, and Alice had fallen asleep before I was halfway done editing, but it was ready.

"So don't worry." Jenn gestured to the pile of props from previous scenes that had been used for the last time. "Help me get these packed up instead."

But I *did* worry, because the film was only part of it. And the other part didn't stand a chance of being ready if Finn couldn't *remember his stupid lines.*

"They're nearly done," Jenn said. "Just ... try to learn patience in the next fifteen minutes and we'll be fine."

Patience?!

Up on the boardwalk, I could hear the music, chanting and stomping of what had to be hundreds and hundreds of protestors – sorry, awareness marchers. They'd obviously finished their first walk along the roads closest to the ocean and would now begin their circuit through the streets of Santa Monica. I checked the time on my phone. They were running late too, at least.

"I need to get up to the hotel." I shoved my phone back in my pocket. "Can you go and, I don't know, mouth the words to Finn from off-camera or something?"

Jenn ignored that request. "You'll be back in time for the thing?"

"Wouldn't miss it," I called back over my shoulder.

I ran into Alice as I raced towards the Oceanfront Hotel.

"Perfect timing," she said with a smile. "Think your mum is already here?"

We pushed open the doors to find several men in tuxedos rearranging the lobby furniture. "I'd say yes."

Mum, it seemed, had changed her mind completely about how she wanted the event to run from our meeting the day before, and now the hotel was scrambling to catch up. We jumped into the fray to start helping – Alice by moving vases of flowers, me by grabbing Mum and taking her away from the glowering hotel staff and over to the room where we were *actually* holding the fundraiser.

"Doesn't it look perfect in here?" I positioned her at the entrance and gestured to the room.

Navy, silver and sea-foam green decorations filled the room – from the dark tablecloths to the biodegradable table confetti to the gauzy green-blue curtains that lined the windows. We'd picked the function room that backed almost directly on to the beach and those windows actually folded back the whole way to the wall, to open up the room to a wooden deck not unlike the one at the Shore Thing, with steps down to the sand.

The tables were each decorated with a driftwood centrepiece, studded with shells and tiny lights. Beach lanterns hung from the ceiling over each table, and nets of fairy lights were strung around the walls, and all around the deck outside. When it got dark later, it was going to be properly magical.

"It looks perfect, Mum."

Mum frowned, looking towards the end of the room. "What's that doing there?"

I followed her gaze and spotted the large screen I'd requested, visible from the deck and the beach beyond as well as the function room itself. "Oh. I imagine they just forgot to put that away..." Dashing across the room, I found the button to make the screen retreat up into its case on the ceiling.

Alice appeared in the doorway. "Oh! It's beautiful."

"Don't you think I should get them to take that screen out altogether, Alice? I don't like that black thing on the ceiling."

"I think it's probably fixed in place, Mum," I said quickly.

"Well, maybe they can cover it then." Mum turned,

obviously looking for a hotel staff member to boss around.

"Oh, actually Mrs Andrews, it could be perfect!" Alice said suddenly. "I mean, we could show some of the photos of the work the Shore Thing Project have been doing this year! Jake and I could put together a slide show."

Mum didn't look entirely convinced. "Do you really think that's appropriate for a fundraiser like this?"

"Letting people see what they're actually raising money for?" I said sarcastically. "No, I wouldn't have thought so."

Mum shot me an exasperated look. "People expect a certain level of sophistication from an event like this, Willa. It's bad enough that I had to pull it together at such short notice, but—"

"I think Darla would really like it," Alice put in. "I mean, she was so determined that today should be about raising awareness. And isn't half the problem with the climate emergency that people *say* they're very concerned about it but then don't *do* anything? This way, we're showing them exactly what they *can* do."

Which was the exact point of the film Alice, Jake, Matty, Jenn and I had spent the last forty-eight hours putting together. Somehow, Alice was getting Mum to go along with our plan by telling the absolute truth.

I really hadn't considered that as an option.

It worked. "Fine. The screen stays, and we'll talk to Darla about it later."

Alice and I shared a triumphant look.

"Now, if everything seems to be in order here, we can go and get ready! I've reserved us girls a suite upstairs. Come on!"

OK, this wasn't in the plan.

"How are we going to work this?" I whispered to Alice as we headed for the lifts.

She bit her lip, thinking hard. Then she smiled. "It's just a shame you take *so* long to get ready, Willa. I mean, you could be *ages* up there. Right?"

"Right," I said, smiling back.

This could all still work. I hoped.

ALICE

Lucky for us, the suite Mrs Andrews had booked turned out to have two bedrooms with en-suite bathrooms, plus a lounge area. Mrs Andrews chose the main bedroom to get ready in, while Willa and I quickly took over the other one and shut the door behind us.

"OK, what are we going to do?" Willa asked, jumping up on to the bed.

I crossed the room and looked out of the window. A metal fire escape lined the wall outside, with stairs all the way down to ground level. Perfect.

"Right," I said, turning back to Willa. "I'm going to stay here and talk to myself while I get changed, and you're going to climb out of the window and go make sure your film crew are still on schedule."

Willa, to her credit, didn't blink at the idea. And I hadn't even told her about the fire escape.

"And then what?"

"I'll tell your mum you're still doing your hair, or whatever. Hopefully that will buy you enough time to get everything sorted then get back here and get changed." I'd seen how long Willa's hair and make-up routine could take. It was perfectly plausible. "But you'd better go fast."

Willa nodded and headed for the window. I headed for the dress bags, and hoped I could stall Mrs Andrews long enough.

"Oh, Alice, you look lovely!" Mrs Andrews said as I emerged from the bedroom. "That sea-foam gown was definitely the right choice for you."

"Thank you. You look beautiful too." Mrs Andrews' navy gown with the silver trim was somehow both classic *and* unique, and she wore it with the confidence that only film stars and Willa seemed to have.

"Where's Willa? I can't *wait* to see her in that silver dress." Mrs Andrews took a step towards our bedroom, and I darted into her path.

"Oh, um, she spent so long helping me with my hair and make-up, she's only just getting changed now," I lied, ignoring the instant pang of guilt in my stomach. "I said I'd come out and start helping you and she can follow us later."

Mrs Andrews looked mollified. I let out a long

breath as she turned back to the hallway.

"I suppose that's OK. And I really do need to get downstairs and check the welcome drinks have all been organized."

I trailed Mrs Andrews down to the hotel lobby, where guests would be welcomed before heading through to the main function room. In most of the hotels I'd stayed in, the lobby had a reception desk, maybe a sofa or two, and perhaps a vending machine and some leaflets about local attractions.

The Oceanside was not that sort of hotel.

The lobby had huge windows all across the back wall, opening up to the beach decking that I imagined must be connected to the function room. The hotel seemed to be more glass than brick, more outside than in. Even the elevators were glass, situated right in the middle of the building and surrounded by lush, green foliage. Potted palm trees were dotted around and, now Mrs Andrews had rearranged the furniture, every seat looked out over the ocean, and there was a long table lined with champagne glasses behind the elevators.

"We'll have waiters circulating with trays too, of course, though, won't we?" Mrs Andrews asked the event planner, who nodded. "Now, what else do we need to check...?"

I trailed around after Willa's mum, doing everything I could to assist, and hoping that she didn't remember that Willa was still upstairs. Eventually though, I ran out of time.

"Oh, Alice! The details for the silent auction. I totally forgot about it! Could you go through them and make sure it's all set up right?" she asked. "The first guests will be arriving soon. Willa knows what to do, she's done them before. She must be ready by now – just go and grab her."

"Of course," I said with a faint smile, thinking frantically. "Um, actually, I need to pop back to the Shore Thing for some … things. But I'll go find Willa and get her working on the silent auction first, before I go."

"OK, sweetheart." I backed away, but Mrs Andrews' attention was already back on the event planner's clipboard, double-checking more details.

As I rode up in the glass elevator, Willa's mum moved towards the back deck, a blur of navy against all the white and glass, only recognizable because of her dress. It was like Willa had said; sometimes, we saw the clothes and just made assumptions about the person wearing them.

That was it!

Racing back towards the suite, I quickly shucked off my beautiful sea-green gown and shimmied into Willa's silver one, promising myself as I did so that this would be the *absolute* last time I pretended to be Willa. Then I quickly pulled my hair up in a style that I hoped looked fancy enough, from a distance. The most important thing was, it didn't look the same as how I was wearing mine earlier.

Hoping I'd done enough, I headed back for the elevator at top speed. As I'd expected, Mrs Andrews and the event planner were still out by the deck. They looked up as the elevator swooped down and I waved, trusting that the distance and the glass would be enough to obscure my facial features a little.

It seemed to work. Mrs Andrews waved back, then pointed towards the small side room where the silent auction was being held. I gave her a thumbs up and she nodded. I held my breath as the lift came to a stop in the lobby. If Mrs Andrews came over to talk to me, she'd see instantly that I wasn't Willa, and the whole thing would be up.

But she didn't. Seemingly satisfied with her instructions to me, she headed out on to the main deck. I heaved a sigh of relief as the doors opened, and raced across the lobby to the silent auction room.

I didn't have long to get things set up there, but how hard could it be?

Any minute now, the next stage of our plan would fire into action. And there was no way I was missing that!

WILLA

I made it back to the beach just as they *finally* wrapped. Being there to hear Fran say the words, "Aaaand … that's a wrap, guys!" followed by the whoop that went up from the cast and crew meant more than I'd thought it would. I felt a real part of the team, even if I hadn't been there the whole time.

We'd made a film. My *first* film as part of a crew. A proper independent short, that would be shown to actual people, once all the editing was done.

It felt good.

But I didn't have long to bask in the feeling.

"Everybody ready?" I asked Jenn. Already I could hear the sounds of singing and chanting from the boardwalk. The awareness marchers were making their way back down along the edge of the beach.

She nodded. "Matty and Tyler are going to finish packing up here while the rest of us get to work. Is the music ready?"

"Should be." If Alice and Jake had done their part right. Taking over the small speaker and microphone

Darla had used for her opening talk and linking it up to Jake's phone had hopefully been straightforward enough.

"Then let's go!"

There were plenty of hugs and congratulations as I handed out the T-shirts Alice and I had customized, staying late at the Shore Thing on Thursday night. Everyone slipped them on as we headed up to join the march.

We caught up with them just past the pier, as they headed towards the Shore Thing headquarters and the Oceanside Hotel. Jake threw me a thumbs up when he spotted me and I smiled, starting to relax at last.

The timing was perfect. This was the busiest part of the boardwalk, with the most tourists there to witness what was about to happen. Already the Shore Thing volunteers seemed to have swelled the number of marchers considerably since they started, and many of the newcomers were clutching leaflets or spare placards that Jake and Alice had made.

The whole thing had a sort of carnival atmosphere, loud and festive and happy, with the bright colours of the Shore Thing shirts people were wearing shining against the bright blue sky. Little kids sat on their parents' shoulders waving jellyfish flags. People seemed … hopeful.

Fran caught my eye and I nodded. It was time.

Raising one hand high above my head, I gave Jake the signal, and suddenly something new boomed through the air.

"This is your captain speaking," Jake said into the microphone, loud enough to draw the attention of everyone in the vicinity. I caught sight of Darla, at the other end of the crowd, turning around in confusion. And standing next to her was… Oh pants. Principal Carter. Well, it was too late now. Jake was on fire. "These are our waves, our oceans, our beaches. It's time to reclaim them. To save them. And it's definitely time to … DANCE!"

The music kicked in at just the right moment, loud and pulsing, the bass making my blood vibrate in my veins. And at exactly the same time, my friends – Fran, Jenn, the cast and crew – sprang into action.

We hadn't had much time to rehearse in between filming, but most of these guys had been performing their whole lives. Fran twirled in first, followed by Polly and Bethany in perfect synchronicity. The crowd started clapping as Derek and Finn joined in, lifting the girls and spinning them, placing them down on the railings for added height.

That was the cue for Jenn, Kat and even me to join

the dance. The crowd made room for us as we all fell into formation, the music carrying me through the steps without even thinking.

Then, as the key changed, it was time for the hardest part. With a quick glance round to make sure the others were doing the same, I reached out into the crowd and grabbed the hands of a stranger, drawing them into the dance. Luckily my partner – a woman a bit older than Mum – was game for anything and copied my steps perfectly.

I grinned with relief as more and more people started dancing with us, barely even seeming to notice as we led them along the boardwalk, step by step.

Jake moonwalked backwards past me, calling, "Where's Alice?" over the music.

"At the hotel, I think," I yelled back. "But she should be watching out for us…"

I spun my partner round so I could see ahead better, and caught a glimpse of shiny silver fabric, almost blinding me in the sunlight.

Jake spotted her at the same moment I did. I could tell because his mouth fell open at the sight. Alice, wearing that incredible silver gown, was dancing her way down the boardwalk.

"Time for stage three!" I said gleefully, and handed

my partner off to another dancer, shimmying my way towards Alice. "You're wearing my dress!"

"Had to pretend to be you," Alice explained. "Come on. We need to get back and changed before this lot reach the hotel."

It would be cutting it close, I knew, to pull it off. But we *had* to be there when the flash mob arrived at the Oceanside – which was exactly when the fundraiser attendees were enjoying their welcome drinks. Not a coincidence.

It was one thing raising awareness around the people and tourists of Santa Monica, Alice had said as she'd explained her plan to me and Jake earlier that week. And it was one thing to get rich celebrities to donate money to the Shore Thing Project.

"But what if we could raise money *and* awareness?" she'd said. "I mean, the donations are important, of course. But if people hand over their money and then keep living exactly the same way they've always done, nothing changes. And people *know* there's a problem. They just need us to tell them what *they* themselves can actually do about it – even if they don't have millions of dollars to donate and an invitation to a swanky fundraiser."

"So we bring them together," Jake had said. "But how?"

And that, of course, was the rest of Alice's plan.

Now, through music and dance and the busiest few days I'd ever lived through, it was happening. Every single person on that awareness march, including the random tourists and locals we'd swept up along the way, was on their way to gatecrash Mum's fundraiser. And we *really* had to get there first.

ALICE

We had a bit of a close call as we reached the hotel and spotted Willa's mum on the deck by the beach, looking out towards the approaching flash mob, but Willa grabbed my arm and yanked me around the side of the hotel before she spotted us. Together we clattered up the fire escape and climbed back into our suite through the open window – harder than it sounds in a floor-length silver dress.

Quickly, we changed – me into my sea-foam gown, and Willa into the silver dress I'd been wearing – and raced down the many flights of stairs to the lobby, not willing to even wait for the elevator.

"Where have you two *been?*" Mrs Andrews asked as we rushed, breathless, into the function room. Already it was filled with people in tuxedos and evening gowns, sipping on champagne cocktails and making polite conversation. One or two of them I *definitely* recognized from the big screen, and I was sure I'd seen plenty of the others before too.

This was Willa's world. And I was about to bring

272

mine crashing right into it.

"Sorry, Mum!" Willa called, already moving past her on to the deck. "Have you seen what's going on out here?"

The flash mob hadn't been that far behind us when we'd started running for the hotel, and now it was here in force, filling the beach below the hotel with music and dancing.

"Are they protesters?" a man nearby asked us, peering down at the signs. "They know we're here to support the same cause as them, right?"

"No!" Willa said, looking at me with wide eyes. It hadn't even occurred to me that people might think that! We needed to get moving with stage four, quickly. "I think they're here in support. To celebrate … ocean awareness?"

"Where's the switch for the screen?" I whispered, and Willa pointed towards the wall opposite.

"You get it down, I'll make sure Matty has loaded the film."

The film had been a labour of love for Willa. For all that she'd skipped out on the first week and half of her volunteering at the Shore Thing Project, she'd been making up for it over the last few days. She'd followed me and Jake around with her camera, learning everything she could about the work the project did. Matty and Jenn had helped too, arriving on set early and staying on the beach after Fran had called it for the day, to get footage of Santa Monica through the day and into the evening. Together with Willa, they'd got plenty of shots of the rubbish left there and the damage it could do, as well as the vibrancy and life the shoreline had – for people and marine life.

Willa had even interviewed Darla in her office, pretending to be me, of course. And then she'd taken some of the existing educational films the project used for school visits and spliced them together with her own footage to make a complete short film, all about the importance of conserving our oceans – and asking the viewer to think about how they could play their part to make it happen.

It might have been rushed and lacking a bit in finesse, filmed without lighting and all the other equipment the crew had used for Willa's *actual* film project – but to my mind it was a masterpiece.

And now it was time to share it with everyone.

I flicked the switch and the huge screen lowered into the room. It was on a special arm that meant we'd been able to flip it out through the open doors so

274

it hung at the edge of the deck, visible to those down on the beach as well as those attending the fundraiser. As it started up, the crowds began to fall silent. Soon, people from the march on the beach, and Willa's film group, had started climbing the steps up on to the deck to watch too, mingling with the rich and famous at the fundraiser. Mostly the invited guests seemed too focused on Willa's film to notice they'd been joined by the awareness marchers.

I stared, amazed to see myself on camera, talking to a group of kids about the beach clean-up they were about to help with. I hadn't even realized Willa had snuck in that afternoon to film me.

Now I glanced across the deck and saw Jake smiling at me. "Superstar," he mouthed, and I ducked my head to hide my smile.

The video came to a close with a gorgeous shot of Santa Monica beach at sunset, and Willa's voiceover asking, "What will you do to save it?" as the music faded out. The crowd burst into applause – but soon, there was another buzz filling the room.

Questions.

It had worked. Everyone was asking what *they* could do, every day, to make a difference. People were asking about single-use plastics, recycling, beach clean-ups, *everything* Willa had mentioned in her film.

The only problem was, they weren't waiting for answers.

I shot a worried look at Jake, but he was already talking with one of the hotel staff who, after a moment, produced a microphone from a concealed cupboard. Jumping up on to the raised area at the end of the deck that functioned as a sort of stage, he spoke into the mic.

"Thanks, everyone, for watching this Shore Thing Project film – and for coming out today to support us!" That got a huge cheer from the crowd. "And I'd especially like to thank Willa Andrews for putting the film together for us. She's the one over there in the silver dress." He pointed in our direction, and Willa took a little bow as another round of applause rippled through the room.

"Now, as we all know, saving our oceans will take effort from every one of us," Jake went on. "And I'd like to invite Shore Thing volunteer, my good friend Alice Wright, up to answer some of your questions."

My eyes widened with horror as I looked up at him. Willa nudged me in the ribs. "Go on. Your turn in the spotlight."

"I can't!" I whispered. "Darla should do it. Or one of the other volunteers."

"Oh, I don't think so," Darla said, suddenly beside me. "Seems to me you've been doing the work of *two* volunteers these last few weeks. I think we can trust you to come up with Shore Thing-approved answers."

Willa looked a little nervous at that, especially as her mum was standing next to Darla.

Looks like the secret was out.

Maybe up on the stage was the safest place to be. Of course, every other time I'd done this, I'd been Willa. Wearing her clothes and her confidence like a costume. A shield.

Now I was just Alice Wright.

I had to do this as me.

Jake handed me the microphone and I stared out at the crowd.

I took a deep breath and started to speak.

"Hello, everyone. I know you must have a lot of questions, and I'm looking forward to answering them all. But first, I have a couple of questions for you. Firstly, how many species do you think live in our oceans. Anyone?"

ALICE

You won't believe what I just did!!

LUCA

If this is anything to do with that Jake guy, I REALLY don't want to know.

ALICE

No! Well, sort of. But not like THAT.

ALICE

I just stood up on stage in front of a room full of celebrities, volunteers and a beach full of awareness marchers, and answered questions about how we can protect our oceans.

ALICE

And I wasn't even pretending to be Willa while I did it.

LUCA

Why would you need to pretend to be Willa? That definitely sounds like an Alice thing to do.

WILLA

Alice was on fire, answering every question articulately and intelligently. Jake chimed in sometimes, and Darla joined them to answer questions about the Shore Thing Project itself, but Alice was definitely the star of the show.

I didn't have my camera with me, but I did whip out my phone to record the moment for posterity. Then, when Alice was done, I made sure I got some footage of the rest of the event too – including the local news crew who had showed up to film.

"I know it can sometimes feel like we're just a tiny fish in a wide ocean," Alice said, "but being honest with ourselves about the way we live our lives isn't nothing. And making those small changes adds up. So start small. Take your reusable coffee cup every time you get a takeaway latte. Bring your own shopping bag. Then, once those things are habit, take on single-use plastics and try to cut them out of your life as far as you can. Get really serious about recycling. Just keep looking for the next small change – and know that every single one makes a difference. And the more people we can persuade to make these changes, the bigger the difference we can make.

"But if you only remember one thing from tonight, remember this: your choices matter. Your decisions count. And you can always, always make a difference."

Applause sounded through the room. I captured Alice's smiling face, then swung around to get a full panorama of the room and found my mum's face filling the screen.

I flipped off the video and tried to smile innocently. Mum raised a disbelieving eyebrow.

"I think it's time we had a little chat. Don't you?"

We headed down to the beach, leaving our heels on the deck and letting our feet sink into the sand as we walked. I wasn't sure where to start, but in the end, I went with the beginning – the day Alice arrived, and the plan we'd devised. Turns out it was far simpler to just tell the whole truth, rather than come up with more lies.

"The point of you volunteering this holiday was to get you thinking about others," Mum pointed out as I finished the story. "Not to con your friend into taking your punishment for you."

"I know," I said miserably, not even bothering to

mention that it had been Alice's idea in the first place. I knew that wasn't the point. "And I mean, it took me a while to figure it out. But I *did* try to make up for it in the end. Not to mention, the Shore Thing Project probably got a better deal out of having Alice there, anyway. Did you see her up there?"

That made Mum smile. "She was brilliant. And so was the film you made." Then she sighed. "But that doesn't change the fact that you lied to me about where you were, what you were doing and who you were with. That's fundamental, Willa. You know our number-one rule."

My parents gave me quite a lot of leeway about how I spent my time, and they knew with their careers that they couldn't keep watch on me all the time, anyway. But the rule was, I had to tell them where I was and who I was with.

And I'd broken it.

"At least I was in the right country this time?" I tried, but Mum's expression didn't change. "I'm sorry, Mum. I really am. And I'll take whatever punishment you decide is right."

"Hmmm." Mum turned back towards the hotel, looking thoughtful. "What do *you* think would be an appropriate punishment?"

I blinked. Me? "Um, I guess, maybe volunteering at the Shore Thing for the rest of the school year?" Beach clean-ups weren't exactly my first choice of a fun way to spend a Saturday, but if I had to be punished it might as well be a *useful* punishment.

"Looks like you might not be the only one." Mum nudged my arm and pointed back towards the Oceanside. There, on the beach, on the deck, and probably inside the room too, stage five of Alice's plan was taking effect. Shore Thing volunteers with clipboards were taking down the details of anyone who wanted to join the ranks, now they knew what was involved.

And they had lines of people waiting to sign up.

I saw Jenn and Fran plus several people in evening gowns in the queues, as well as many of the casual marchers we'd picked up along the way.

It had worked. And even if it meant I'd be picking up litter from the beach for the rest of my school career, it was worth it.

I beamed and Mum smiled back.

"Come on, you. Let's get back to the party. Don't forget, it's Alice's last night. Let's all celebrate together."

ALICE

The fundraiser was such a magical night that I could almost have forgotten I'd be leaving for London the next day. But as the crowds started to thin out, I couldn't pretend any longer.

My time in LA was almost over.

I stood there in the middle of the beautifully decorated room and let the events of the last two weeks sink in.

"Hey, you. You were fantastic up there tonight." Jake appeared from the deck, his hands in his pockets, smiling at me.

"Thanks for pushing me up there," I said, crossing towards him. "I wouldn't have done it on my own."

"I know," he said simply. "But I knew you'd be amazing at it, so..." He shrugged.

"And I'm sorry we didn't have much time for our date," I added.

"That's OK. This was more important."

There was an awkward pause as we just stared at each other. Then I blurted out the words I knew we were both thinking.

"I'm leaving for London in the morning. I don't know if I'll ever come back to LA."

"Maybe I'll come to London, one day," Jake said. "And until then … it would be great to stay in touch."

"Definitely," I said, smiling. "I'm so grateful I got to know you, Jake. Thank you. You've helped me … find myself again."

"I'm glad." He moved closer, meeting my gaze then pulling me into a hug. "Because I think you're incredible."

"You're pretty incredible too," I murmured against his shoulder. "Even if you do eat burgers from the stand with the non-recyclable packaging."

He laughed into my hair. "No one's perfect."

He pulled back then, just enough to look into my eyes again. Whatever he saw there obviously convinced him, because he leaned in slowly and kissed me – soft and sweet, like in a movie. The perfect end to my LA adventure.

"Goodbye, Alice," he murmured as he let me go. And then he walked away, leaving me still smiling.

Back at Willa's house, we all changed out of our fancy dresses and into our PJs, and Willa and her mum debated which movie to watch for my last night and whether we had enough popcorn.

Leaving them to it, I slipped out to sit by the pool and video-call my dad.

"Starfish! How's it all going over there in La La Land? We can't wait to have you home again tomorrow."

Home. I was ready to head back, I thought. But hearing the word made me think again about the house they'd chosen without me. "I'm looking forward to seeing you too," I said. "Although I'll miss Willa, and working at the Shore Thing Project." And Jake, I thought but didn't say. Some things a dad doesn't need to know.

"I'm sure you will. But hopefully Willa can come over in the summer? We should have moved into the new house before the wedding, so there'll be plenty of room for her to stay."

"I looked through the photos Mabel sent over," I told him. "The house looks nice."

It *did* look nice – it looked like a happy house. But I wouldn't know that for sure until I'd actually seen it myself.

Except ... if I was there with Dad and with Mabel,

how could it be anything else? When the three of us were together, we *were* happy.

The house was just the building we'd put that happiness in.

"I'm so glad you like it," Dad said, relief clear in his expression. "I worried, because you didn't mention it much whenever you called. And Mabel said all along that we shouldn't put an offer in without you seeing it. But I didn't want to lose it and it just felt ... right. You know?"

"I'm sure I'll love it when I see it," I said, hoping it was true.

"Well, we've arranged for you to visit it with us the day after you get back," Dad said. "And if you don't like it, we can still pull out."

"If you and Mabel say it's right for us, then I trust you," I told him. "I can't wait to see it. But the important thing is that we'll all be there together."

"Exactly," Dad said, smiling. "And we'll decorate your room, of course. Once we have all our things in there it'll feel much more ours, don't you think?"

"Of course it will," I replied, suddenly more confident.

"We miss you, Starfish. Hurry home."

Home.

London was home, now. Dad and Mabel were home. The new house was home.

And suddenly I realized what that meant.

I had to stop hiding from my new life there – hiding in the library, the girls' toilets, at the back of the class. I had to start *living* there. Making friends – even just letting Hal be more of a friend would be a start.

Small changes, one at a time. Like taking a reusable coffee cup – or, in this case, talking to someone new. Spending lunch in the canteen or the playground, not the library.

I didn't need to be Willa in London. I needed to be me – the Alice who could stand on stage and tell people important things. The one who cared about the world, the environment, other people. And the one who knew how to have *fun*.

That was the Alice I was taking home to London.

WILLA

"I can't believe you're leaving in the morning," I whispered to Alice as we snuggled down into our beds later that night.

"I know," she murmured. "It's gone so fast!"

"You had a good time though?"

"The best," she replied, and I could see her grin in the light from my alarm clock, set for early in the morning, ready to catch her flight. "Do you think your mum will let you come over to London for the wedding this summer?"

I considered this. It was only a few months away now, I'd need to get working on Mum. I'd let her down this holiday, I knew, but I also thought I'd gone a way to making up for it too. "I reckon I can persuade her."

"Good. It wouldn't be the same without you there."

"Of course it wouldn't." I flopped on to my back and smiled at the ceiling. "Nothing ever is."

She laughed at that, which was why I'd said it, of course.

"Plus you'll need my help to pick the bridesmaids' dresses," I went on. "Otherwise you'll end up with some sort of sea-creature-themed outfits. And fish in the bouquet or something."

Alice laughed louder, burying her face in her pillow so Mum didn't hear us and come tell us to get to sleep.

"I think Mabel has *slightly* better taste than that," she said, when she'd recovered.

"Are you sure? Because I've been shopping with her…"

When Alice's giggles finally subsided, I asked her the question I'd been dying to ask all evening. "So, how was it?"

"How was what?" she asked, sounding confused.

I rolled my eyes, even though she probably couldn't see me in the dark. "Kissing Jake!"

"Oh! That." I knew she was blushing, just from her voice. "It was … nice."

"Just nice?"

"OK, fine. It was perfect."

After we'd dissected Alice's first kiss to pieces, neither of us could sleep. Instead, we chatted about everything and nothing until late in the night, when Alice dropped off mid-sentence, leaving me alone with my thoughts.

It hadn't been *exactly* the spring break I'd imagined when I invited Alice over to LA for the holiday. But in lots of ways it had been better.

Eventually, I fell asleep, still smiling.

ALICE

We all slept late the next morning, Willa's alarm clock failing to wake us, and in the end it was a rush to get me and my suitcase – hastily filled with what I hoped were all my belongings, and possibly a few of Willa's as well – to the airport on time.

We made it though. Willa and Mrs Andrews saw me to the gate, and we all hugged goodbye before I was handed over to the Unaccompanied Minors person.

"I'll see you in London for the wedding though, right?" I said to Willa, glancing nervously at Mrs Andrews for approval as I remembered our conversation the night before. Willa had been certain she could convince her mum, but I was less sure.

"Definitely!" Willa said. "Right, Mum?"

Mrs Andrews gave a long-suffering smile. "We'll talk to your dad. But if you can manage to stay out of trouble that long…"

Oh. If that was the criteria, we had no chance. My face fell and Mrs Andrews laughed.

"OK, I'm sure she can. I'll talk to Mabel and your dad, Alice, and we'll figure it all out."

"Great!" I hugged Willa again one last time.

I was almost at the security gate when Willa yelled after me. I spun quickly, to try to catch her words before I was carried away by the mass of people trying to catch their flights.

"Check your phone!" she called, one hand cupped around her mouth. "Before you take off. I'm sending you something!"

Because I was so late, I practically had to run for the gate, the Unaccompanied Minors rep looking very stressed as he jogged beside me. But then the plane sat on the runway for ages, so I had time to download the video Willa had sent me. The still image it showed was of the room at the Oceanside the night before. Putting in my ear buds, I pressed play, and watched as the camera turned to me and Jake up on stage, and I heard my own voice speaking.

I pulled a face as I listened – I've never liked hearing my own voice recorded – but then I stopped paying attention to the sound of my voice and started listening to the words I was saying.

"But if you only remember one thing from tonight, remember this: your choices matter. Your decisions count.

And you can always, always make a difference."

The camera swung around the room, taking in my audience, the decorations, and even the marchers out on the deck and the beach. The microphone picked up all the applause as I finished speaking.

Now, on the plane, I touched my fingers to my mouth and remembered my first kiss. Maybe I'd never see Jake again. But I knew I wouldn't forget him – or the way he'd made me feel.

Like I could do anything. Even if I was just Alice Wright.

The plane took off and I snuggled down ready to doze some more. At the other end, I knew that Dad and Mabel would be waiting for me. And on Tuesday I'd be back at my new school. And even though I didn't have any real friends there yet, I knew I could make some. Just like we could make the new house our home.

When the plane landed, I'd be back in London, and I knew that it would be good to be home again.

It would be good to be *me* again.

ACKNOWLEDGEMENTS

I have had so much fun writing Alice and Willa's adventures, that it only seems right to thank all the people who made it possible:

- My agent, Gemma Cooper, always
- My incredible editor, Ruth Bennett. Every book we've worked on together has been a hundred times better for her involvement.
- Everyone else at Stripes for all their enthusiasm and hard work in bringing this book to life. Most especially:
  - Ella Whiddett, editor
  - Emma Young, copyeditor
  - Lisa Morris, cover designer
  - Sophie Bransby, designer
  - Leilah Skelton, marketing and publicity
  - Melissa Hyder, proofreader.
- My family and friends, for their unwavering support. Particular thanks to my husband, Simon, and my children, Holly and Sam, who have to live

with me when I'm deep in revisions or stressing over edits.

But most of all, I'd like to thank *you*. For picking up this book out of all the books you could have chosen to read. For coming with me – and Alice and Willa – on this new adventure. For believing in my stories, recommending them to friends, reviewing them online and just taking them into your lives and your hearts. *You* are who I wrote this book for. I hope you loved it.

Have you read?

KATY CANNON

THE SWITCH UP

TWO FRIENDS. ONE SUMMER.
MAJOR DRAMA!

WILLA
Drama queen
Fashion guru
Spontaneous
Looks like Alice

ALICE
Bookworm
Allergic to fashion
Planner
Looks like Willa

LAX Departure Lounge.
Two girls board the same flight to London
as complete strangers. When the plane touches down,
it's the beginning of the craziest plan ever.
Can Willa and Alice really swap lives for the summer?
Things are going to get complicated...

ABOUT THE AUTHOR

Katy was born in Abu Dhabi, grew up in Wales,
went to university in Lancaster, then spent a few years
splitting her time between London, Hertfordshire
and an assortment of hotels across the world. She now
lives in a little market town not far from Cambridge.
She has a husband, two children, a goldfish and far too
many notebooks. As a teenager, Katy was constantly in
trouble for reading when she should have been doing
something else. These days, she mostly gets in trouble
for dreaming up new stories when she should be
writing the ones she's already working on.

www.katycannon.com
@KatyJoCannon